"There exist on Kregen as well as Earth bone-dry pundits who scorn tales of adventure. If these people lack the breadth of imagination to encompass an understanding of the pressures on, condition of, illumination of and triumphs and failures of the human spirit then that is their loss, not ours. The unwillingness to accept defeat tamely does not brand a person as a monster—it may, of course. But then, that is what adventure tends to do, sort the sheep from the goats, the ponshoes from the leems, make people face themselves, shorn of pretensions, and—perhaps, if they are lucky—grasp at a little of what the human spirit exists at all for. . . ."

—DRAY PRESCOT

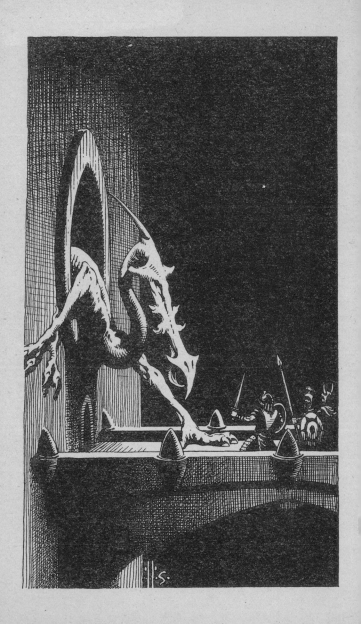

MAZES
OF
SCORPIO

by
Dray Prescot

As told to
ALAN BURT AKERS

DAW BOOKS, INC.
DONALD A. WOLLHEIM, PUBLISHER
1633 Broadway, New York, NY 10019

FIRST PRINTING, JUNE 1982

1 2 3 4 5 6 7 8 9

 DAW TRADEMARK REGISTERED
U.S. PAT. OFF. MARCA
REGISTRADA. HECHO EN U.S.A.

PRINTED IN U.S.A.

TABLE OF CONTENTS

A NOTE ON THE PANDAHEM CYCLE

Dray Prescot often calls himself a plain sailorman, yet the picture he paints of himself in these narratives is highly enigmatic. In *Mazes of Scorpio*, the first volume of the Pandahem Cycle, a completely new era in his life begins to develop. True, he was a powder monkey in Nelson's Navy, and clawed his way through the hawsehole to the quarterdeck to become first lieutenant of a seventy-four. But he was disappointed with his posting. When the Savanti, those mortal yet superhuman people of the Swinging City of Aphrasöe on far Kregen, called him to serve as a Savapim in their schemes, he crossed the gulf of four hundred light-years more than willingly.

Rejected by the Savanti, he in turn spurned them for the sake of Delia. Only through the machinations of the Star Lords was Prescot brought back to Kregen. He has fought his way on that marvelous and brilliant world of savagery and beauty, and has made a name for himself. But now all that changes.

Called to be the Emperor of Vallia, he, with his comrades, has vanquished poor old mad Thyllis, Empress of Hamal, and now seeks to create a fresh and lasting unity among all the nations of Paz. They all face a common foe in the Shanks, the Fishheads who raid their coasts. And, there are worms within the bud, secret enemies who desire only to drag all down for their own selfish ends.

Dray Prescot has been described as an immensely broad-shouldered man of enormous vitality, a little above middle height, with brown hair and eyes, a man conveying an impression of passion held in check, moving with the savage grace of a wild beast of the jungle. From sources outside his own testimony we know him to be a man of complete integrity, holding within himself a cool center of calm; a passionate, dominant, commanding and yet truly humble man.

7

Prescot is chivalrous—in what many people would see as a comically old-fashioned way—to any woman deserving of chivalry. He acknowledges, and tolerates and attempts to be sympathetically understanding toward, any woman who is not.

A plain sailorman? Hardly. Life on Kregen under the mingled streaming lights of Zim and Genodras, the Suns of Scorpio, has changed and matured Prescot in ways unknowable to denizens of this Earth. We can guess that his headlong career has barely begun, that the many friends and foes surrounding him, the horrendous experiences he has endured, the future perils he must face, will continue to mold his character, hardening what is already harsh, softening what is already gentle. All we can say is—Hai Jikai!

                                                      Alan Burt Akers

Chapter One

At The Ruby Winespout

At the beginning of rhododendron time two of my spies were fished out of the river with their throats cut from ear to ear.

The banked masses of leaves, black-green and shining, burst—it seemed in the course of a single morning—into explosions of color. The blossoms scattered flecks and rushes, swathes and coruscations of all the colors of the rainbow across the dark green leaves. Color rioted and scents perfumed the air. And two good men were dead.

Anger and self-contempt were useless. Anger at the waste of human life, contempt that I had asked Nogan the Artful and Lifren the Soft to spy for me; and now they were dead. I told my friends what I intended to do. Their reactions were predictable.

"No!"

"It is impossible."

"You cannot go running headlong into danger!"

But Seg Segutorio, regarding me with his mocking gaze much modified by thought, said, "You probably need to let some of the bad humor out, Dray. Your blood is getting thick. We'll just toddle along to this infamous Ruby Winespout and exercise our muscles a trifle."

Good old Seg!

"And our brains."

"Oh, aye," said Seg. "Brains." His fey blue eyes regarded me with amusement, clearing both mockery and thought. "Between us, we've not used our quota all that well, have we?"

I was surprised.

In all the concerns pressing in on us as we sought to assist a shattered empire to regain its strength with one hand and with the other repel fishlike marauders from over the curve

9

of the world, I had thought Seg secure. He had overcome his
grief for his wife Thelda and was now, I was convinced, the
most balanced of us all. Except and despite that he could become a wild and raving maniac if he got into a spot of
hand-to-hand. As the best Bowman of Loh in all Kregen, in
my view, Seg Segutorio could handle himself in any situation.
He was a comrade, the greatest comrade any man could
have, and I relied on him absolutely.

"I don't know what you're on about for yourself, Seg. But
if you're referring to the bother I'm having with Drak over
this emperor of Vallia nonsense—"

He interrupted with the ease of valued friendship.

"No troubles you can put a shaft into. I've managed to
steer clear of half a dozen designing families with marriage-
able offspring. Since Thelda—well, Dray, I'll tell you. I feel
like those flowers out there."

So that was it.

We were standing in the long room with the serried windows overlooking a panorama of gardens dropping away to
the River Havilthytus. The imperial palace, the Hammabi el
Lamma, rearing imposingly on its artificial island in the river,
had now become a place I could tolerate. The profusion of
flowers helped, for the place always struck cold and hard.
Delia had with her usual skill contrived comfort from the
rooms of the apartments in the Alshyss Tower given over to
our use.

Here in Ruathytu, the capital city of the Empire of Hamal,
we people of Vallia were never allowed to forget we were
strangers. We had concluded a magnificent treaty with the
Hamalese and their new emperor, Nedfar, and everything
looked promising for the future. We had to patch the empire
together again for the Hamalese, and resist with the last drop
of blood in our bodies the devilish Shanks who raided us all.

Seg shifted his belt on his hips, settled it. He coughed.
"The problem now is those rogues in The Ruby Winespout.
They are a notorious gang—"

"So we'll stroll along, as you suggest, and take a look."

The protests from our people, the vehemence with which
this hero and that vowed he or she would accompany us—
well, I cut all through the babble.

"This is a task for one or two only. Kov Seg and I will go.
That is all there is to say."

Deft-fingered Minch, crusty, bearded, my camp commandant, said dourly, "Majister—if the Empress Delia were here she would stop you, for a certainty."

"Well, Minch," I said, somewhat testily, "as she is gallivanting off somewhere and is not here, she can hardly stop me, can she?"

So that decided *that*.

We were going deliberately to put our fool heads into a tavern notorious for murder, foul play and evanishments, where two of our best men had been cruelly done away with, and Seg and I tended to regard it all rather lightly.

We kitted ourselves up to look like mercenaries. This was not a disguise, for we'd both been mercenaries in our time. Our clothes were hard, sober, workmanlike, with much leather and a little metal, for we did not wish to appear grand.

Seg picked up the silken cords from which dangled the representation of a mortil's head sculpted in silver. The ferocious snarling hunting-beast's head looked devilish life-like, a miniature head of destruction. This mortilhead, the pakmort, signified that its wearer was a paktun, a mercenary who had gained fame and notoriety, who perhaps controlled his own free-lance band, although that was more likely to be found among the wearers of the pakzhan, the hyr-paktuns.

"If you like, Seg," I said. "A paktun wearing the pakmort will receive better service than a simple paktun."

"All the same. . . . I don't fancy a knife in my back."

"I agree. You are wise not to wear your pakzhan. The glitter of gold at your throat might tempt a blade."

So, in the end, we hung the silken cords of the pakmorts around our necks and secured the cords to our shoulder points. No mercenary likes an enemy to grip a cord around his neck and choke him to death. Then, flinging short blue-grey capes over our left shoulders and pulling our floppy hats low over our eyebrows, we set off.

We elected to fly saddle birds from the palace.

"We'll have to stable them in a commercial scratching bar establishment," said Seg. "Before we get anywhere near The Ruby Winespout."

"True. One wonders if they'd steal 'em to sell as saddle flyers, or steal 'em to roast and feast on."

The two saddle birds flew strongly through the late afternoon air. We flew high over the river and slanted down toward the southeast, leaving the Sacred Quarter to our rear. We flew over the Blind Walls and the little creek beyond. Ahead a maze of streets and alleyways surrounded the

Eastern Arena. Here lay the homes and hovels of the working folk, the guls, who yet prided themselves they were far better off than the great mass of the clums, who although free and not slave were poor beyond poverty.

Work on the new aqueduct bringing water from the southeast had halted during the recent wars. There were signs around the piles of stones that the building would soon begin again. Like any civilized city of Kregen, Ruathytu consumed vast quantities of water.

We flew down well short of our destination and stabled the two fluttrells; inconspicuous saddle birds, fluttrells, in Ruathytu. The scratching-bar establishment appeared clean and honest. We set off walking in the last of the light from the twin suns.

The street—Seg said he was sure it was the Street of a Thousand Strangers—wore a faded look, with many of the shops and houses shuttered. The skyline was broken here by the looming overhang of the aqueduct, broken sharply at the point where construction had ceased. The clouds hovered overhead, tinged with crimson and jade. Shadows faded and disappeared and then grew again, hard-edged, twinned shadows from the roofs and walls.

"Well, my old dom," said Seg. "And there it is."

The Street of a Thousand Strangers—if that was its name—opened into a small kyro and the square contained the last of a small outdoor conjuring act packing up. They had evidently not attracted much of a crowd. The fire-eater was disconsolately quenching his little brazier. A lady with spangles and not much else to cover her embonpoint stood with a little dark-haired fellow counting the takings.

Seg laughed. "They'd better be off with their gold before night falls."

"Aye!"

Some jugglers slammed the wicker lids on baskets no doubt containing balls and hoops they could spin with dazzling skill. A little breeze whisked leaves and dust. Seg's nod indicated the tavern across the square. A single tree grew outside, a wilting, drooping, yellowish tree. The tavern was built of grey brick, well-weathered and mortared, and the windows were small and mean. It did not look an inviting place.

Seg's nod, besides singling out this dolorous building, stiffened my resolve. The dump looked the kind of place to pass in a hurry and not look back. A shuttered house stood to its right side, and on its left an open space still showed the rotted teeth of a demolished building.

No reason, apart from the unfavorable aspect of this place, should have made me feel a breeze of alarm.

Seg started across.

I followed.

The smell? The feel of that little breeze? This place was wrong.

For all that feeling, I was determined and knew Seg shared my determination that we would not be overawed. We were out for a spot of enjoyment. If spying came into it, all well and good. But we'd been rusting for too long after the tremendous battles in which we'd managed to defeat and, for the moment at least, drive off the hateful marauding Shanks. Those Fishheads from the other side of Kregen were the menace for the future. Right now Seg and I were a couple of harum-scarum mercenaries, out for a night on the town.

Seg Segutorio, who hails from Erthyrdrin, is a wild fey brand of fellow, with black hair and bonny blue eyes, feckless and reckless and, with that otherworldliness of his people, shrewd and canny when he has to be. He and I had adventured a very great deal since Seg had first hurled a forkful of dungy straw into my face. I would not be without Seg for—well, for practically anything at all in two worlds.

As so often occurred, Seg must have picked up the empathy of my feelings, for as we approached the door he said, "Now if Inch and Turko were here, and—"

"Aye," I said.

There was no need to lament between us the absence of our comrades. They had their work to do on Kregen, as we had ours.

A smell of roasting ordel reached us as we strode up the steps to the door. The smell of cooking was good. I cocked an eyebrow at Seg and he nodded, firmly.

"I am sharp set."

So, as we entered the low-ceiled taproom, looking around at tables and chairs positioned about the sawdusted floor, we wrinkled our noses, sniffing the aromas. To the smell of roasting meat was now added the divine scent of fresh momolams.

A man with only three arms wiped his three hands on his blue and yellow striped apron. His jowly face and lemon-shaped head bobbed.

"Welcome, horters, welcome. You are hungry? We have

the best meal this side of the River Mak. Come in, come, and sit down. Hey, Fluffi! Wine for the horters."

At his call a little serving wench came up with feline grace, carrying a pitcher. If that was the wine, they were rough and ready here.

"A middling stuvan, tart," advised the little Och, wiping his three hands again. "But suitable. Oh, yes, suitable."

As Seg and I sat down with our backs to the wall, Seg grumbled, "Anyone would think he was expecting us."

"Trade is bad. We are two paktuns with gold. But what you suggest is worth considering."

"So? How do we consider it?"

"For a start—do we trust the wine?"

"A middling stuvan? Hard to judge."

I laughed. Oh, yes, I can laugh.

"If we don't we'll be thirsty, and suspect—"

"And if we do we could be stuffed down in the cellars, with our throats slit, ready to go out into the river."

"Pre-unfortunately-cisely."

Seg slumped back against the wall and eyed with a most baleful stare the wine the little Fristle fifi had poured for him. I picked up my goblet.

"I'll drink, Seg. You may claim indisposition, religion, temperance—"

"Why you? Why me!"

"You may rearrange the plan, should you wish."

He stared at me.

In a low, a very low voice against eavesdroppers, he said, "You, Dray Prescot, as I have said, are a low-down, devious, cunning, rascal of a devil!"

And I laughed again.

"Landlord!" I called it out between laughs.

He appeared, the apron twisting around two of his hands, the third fidgeting with the table arrangements. "Horters?"

"Would you fetch a fresh bottle of Farfaril, for we have just enough silver between us to pay for a decent wine and our meal." I spoke casually but with emphasis. "After that we will have a pair of copper obs between us."

"At once, horters." He did not sound disappointed.

Although he was a cripple, having only three arms, he was deft enough in removing the two goblets of the stuvan. Farfaril is a full-bodied red wine, not too sweet. I am not over-fond of the wines of Hamal, although a few of their top vintages are superb by any standards.

The little Fristle fifi brought the bottle of Farfaril. It was brought quickly enough, the dust still upon it, and the seals intact. I judged there would not have been time to tamper with it. If it had been drugged ahead of time, and laid by, in store to wreak a mischief, Seg and I would have lost our gamble. . . .

The tavern began to fill up as the twin suns sank beyond the Walls of Repentence. The jugglers came in to spend what little they had earned. A man with a chained Munfoon, all hair and eyes and lolling tongue, came in to make the poor creature dance to the sound of a pipe. The girl who played the pipe was clad in mere rags, her naked feet raw and red, her face a pinched white blot. The Munfoon danced a little jig and a rattle of copper obs fell about the girl. She snatched them up, and together with the man and the chained pathetic creature shuffled to a dark corner. All evening other entertainers would perform their shows. Some were better not spoken of.

There was no doubt about it. The roast ordel and the yellow momolams were superb. We ate hugely. Our silver insured us good helpings and a second bottle. We sat, watching, waiting for the arrival of the man or woman who had caused the deaths of our two spies.

We had chosen our own dark corner, against the walls. There was a certain amount of horseplay—leeming, Kregens call it—and one or two fights. Only one dagger was used, and that only inflicted a minor wound. The blood was mostly from a slashed scalp, and scalps bleed like broken hearts.

"I suppose your information was reliable, Dray?"

"We thought so. That great rogue Hamdi the Yenakker told us. He swore the man to see was regularly here in The Ruby Winespout. A man with three black pigtails, a nose bent to larboard, and missing his left ear."

"If true, bizarre enough to spot."

"We thought so."

"Well, Hamdi did help us before. He would turn his colors the moment a new lord appeared. How long do we give this fellow with the pigtails and the bent nose and the missing lughole?"

"As long as it takes."

"By the Veiled Froyvil, my old dom! And to maintain our cover we've ordered two bottles, and two bottles only. It will be thirsty work."

And this time we both laughed.

"As for the woman, Hamdi was less precise. Not a serving wench, not a shishi, yet a girl who would come here. With a sword strapped to her waist. And coiled hair. Not an easy mark."

"If she does come here, we'll know her."

The first bottle emptied.

We both felt fine.

We started in on the second bottle.

On Earth, where I was born, and which was some four hundred light-years away, a tavern like this would have been wreathed in tobacco smoke. Thankfully, there were no smokers on Kregen.

At least, not tobacco smokers. . . .

A nasty little fight broke out two tables along, and a fellow was carried out feet first and hurled on his head onto the cobbles outside.

The victor, breathing hard, sat back at his bench.

"Stupid tapo! As though one could not see his dice were obviously loaded."

Another man joined them, flicking his little rods of many colors. If he cheated, he was not discovered as the game of Flick-Flock proceeded with much swearing and bangings of the tables.

Seg looked at the clepsydra perched on a shelf above the door. The water dropped steadily. It was a dark lustrous green.

"If he does not come soon, my old dom, my tongue will begin to crawl about seeking sustenance among the tankards."

"Maybe we could discover, with cries of joy, another few silver pieces?"

"Why not?"

In the manner of old campaigners we had automatically appraised the metal of the roisterers and swaggerers in the wide main room of The Ruby Winespout. Rough artisans, mostly, with tradespeople sitting together along the angled wall to our corner. Three tables along, past the gamblers at Flick-Flock, the five men sitting with their heads together had not escaped our notice. We kept a quick glance on them from time to time. They were not artisans or tradesfolk; they carried weapons and three of the five wore brigandines, the other two wore jacks.

"Hey, Landlord!" exclaimed Seg, half-rising and extending his hand. "Lookit that! A real beautiful silver sinver graced with the head of the Empress Thyllis, no less." He puffed his cheeks, and added: "The late Empress Thyllis."

The little och trotted over, looking pleased.

"Late or not, horter, it is all good silver."

"Aye! Another bottle!"

From the corner of my eye, my attention centered amusedly on Seg's antics, I caught movement approaching from the tradespeople's tables. Seg was bellowing: "Caught in the lining! Foul stitching by a half-blind wight, I don't doubt, but I'd kiss his bald pate for him now!"

The movement from my side abruptly manifested itself.

An exceedingly large and extraordinarily hairy man fairly hurtled at me. He knocked over an intervening table. He was purple of face, bulging of eye, foaming of mouth, and screeching something like: "I'll have your tripes out and strangle your scrawny neck in 'em, so help me Uldor the Mighty!"

There was time to observe he wore a shaggy old pelt-like garment, by its bulk probably concealing armor beneath, before he hit our table. Seg toppled away, with his catlike grace recovering instantly. I leaned away from the blow of a ham-sized fist. I dodged. I shouted.

"What the—?"

The hairy mass shoved the table away. The remains of our bottle splashed. The fist swung again, and the maniac roared out: "I know you, Planath the Sly! Now you have reached the reckoning." He lashed out again.

I dodged.

"I'm not—"

"Stand still, Planath, rast, yetch! I am going to scrunch your scrawny neck between my hands! I, Dahram the Bold! Accept your just punishment like a man, cramph!"

He got himself entangled in the wreckage of the table. He kicked out, stumbling, windmilling his arms. He had just the two arms, and was an apim like me, a member of Homo sapiens. But he was large, and hairy, and wrought up. There were precious few options left open to me, by Zair!

His purple face and bulging eyes bore down again. He did not have three black pigtails, his nose was not bent to larboard and his ears were both present and correct.

"Now as Uldor the Mighty is my witness, I have sworn to take payment out on your hide, Planath the Sly! Now is your hour of doom—"

He stopped bellowing rather suddenly.

This was mainly because I placed a hand around his throat and pressed a little. My other hand caught his left arm and bent it back—not cruelly, not viciously, just enough to make him stoop very smartly and rub that squashed and fiery nose against the edge of the overturned table.

I spoke into his ear.

"I am not Planath the Sly, Dahram!"

He grunted. I eased the pressure.

He spluttered. "I know you are not Planath the Sly! He could never do what you have just done! My apologies, dom, sincere apologies—but that physiognomy of yours—"

Seg laughed.

"That'll teach you to monkey with nature!"

Seg knew that I could make subtle adjustments to my face, after a fashion taught me by a famed Wizard of Loh. I'd altered my own fierce features into what I thought would be a face that would not upset Seg too much. I must have put in too much of the sly look.

I let Dahram the Bold up.

He rubbed his throat and eyed me. He was a fine tall bulky man. There was indeed armor under the pelt. His sword was scabbarded into a plain leather sheath, bronze-bound.

The little fracas had loosened the shaggy pelt at his throat. I caught the glitter of gold.

I said, "Cover your pakzhan, Dahram. We do not wear ours here—"

"Aye," said Dahram. "But I sold my pakmort when I became a hyr-paktun, sold it to the brotherhood."

We righted the table and, as though he'd been waiting for the outcome of the little fracas, the Och landlord appeared with the bottle paid for with Seg's sinver he claimed he'd found lodged in his lining.

Dahram the Bold cocked a bushy eyebrow at me.

"Join us, dom, and tell us your story. I own I would not relish being in the shoes of this Planath the Sly."

We were fated not to drink that third bottle of Farfaril.

The five men at the table we'd been casually observing chose that moment to make their move.

As I have said, only one dagger had flashed in the fights so far.

These five men descended on us with naked steel.

The patrons of The Ruby Winespout drew themselves away. Some looked. Most went on with what they were doing, only sparing a glance to see how the fight would go, making their wagers on the outcome. Murder and mayhem occurred too commonly in The Ruby Winespout to raise an alarm.

And, all this in defiance of the strict Laws of Hamal. . . .

I did not think Dahram the Bold was the betrayer, delivering the metaphorical kiss of betrayal by his antics. The five opened out as they rushed along the cleared space before the tables. One of them pushed his enveloping hood away from his face in order to see better. And, lo! He had three black pigtails, and a nose bent to larboard, and only one ear. And, lo! again. One of the five men was a woman, with coiled hair under a steel cap, and a sword which was now a bar of glitter in her gloved fist.

"So that's the way of it!" quoth Seg.

Dahram the Bold didn't waste time. He ripped his sword free of that plain scabbard. The sword was the straight cut and thrust weapon of Havilfar, the thraxter. The swords swinging against us were thraxters, also. There were no rapiers and no main gauches in evidence in this tavern brawl.

Seg and I drew. Now we happened to have strapped on drexers, the superior sword type developed in our home of Valka, a blend of the best aspects of the thraxter, the native Vallian clanxer, and the superb and mysterious Savanti sword. Without another word, we set to.

Chapter Two

Of Beggars and Emperors

In a tavern fight of this brawling nature you don't have to be too choosy. You don't stand on ceremony. The romantic flicker of glittering blades is all very well, but. . . .

The broken bottle rolled at the side of my boot.

I picked the bottle up, noticed that the end was broken into a satisfyingly jagged array of teeth, and gestured with it in my left hand as though I were about to throw it.

The leading wight rushing upon us dodged. He moved his head and shoulders back to avoid the throw. I waited until he'd moved, was fixed at the end of his balance—and then I threw.

The jagged end chewed up his face.

Dahram the Bold hurled himself forward, all bulk and hair, yelling. His sword flickered.

When you are a brand new young prince, or a brand new young emperor, you will find many people only too willing to patronize you, suck up to you, toady, flatter, all in the best interests of your goodself, of course. I had a quick feeling of regret that, for all this hairy magnificence, there had not been a few more men like Dahram the Bold about some of the emperors and kings I'd known. He had assaulted and insulted me; now he did not waste words but just got stuck in to help to redress the balance.

He fought with a panache that overbore the next two assailants. He foined with the thraxter, using the blade as though it were a pea stick. The man with the three black pigtails lost two of them, and half his face with them, as Dahram slashed. The woman turned and ran. The last of the five stood looking with stupid, bewildered eyes at the hilt of the sword. The blade was through his neck. Seg can throw a blade, too, as well as loose a shaft. . . .

As a fight, it was all over almost before it had begun.

"Friends of yours, doms?"

"No, Dahram. Never seen 'em before."

Seg said, "It would seem our journey has been in vain. And the bottle is broken—"

"Yes," I said. "All right, we'll go."

Seg hitched up his belt.

I said to Dahram, "You will take a stoup with us at a more salubrious tavern? We are in your debt."

"For that little bit of knockabout?"

"For disconcerting those damned assassins."

Seg hauled his sword free. He had to put his foot on the dead man's face. "You've seen them before?"

"No," said Dahram. "No. I don't know 'em. I'm tazll at the moment, looking for a job. I heard a merchant will hire guards here."

"There are many taverns where guards are hired."

"True. Very well. And the first drink is on me."

"Are there any sweeter words in any tongue?" quoth Seg.

On that cheerful note we left The Ruby Winespout. No doubt the little crippled Och would have regular arrangements for disposing of dead bodies.

My thoughts became grim. My two spies had been disposed of, their bodies found in the river. . . .

We told Dahram we were called Nath the Hammer and Naghan the Fletcher; but he did not believe us. That did not bother me. Dahram, as I thought, was a chance acquaintance, fine company for an evening on the town away from the Sacred Quarter where the nobles and the gilded youth of the city played. He would sign on as a guard with a merchant and be off in a couple of days. . . .

We swaggered across the square where the jugglers had performed their tricks during the day. We kept a very sharp lookout for the woman who had run off. The way I saw the situation was spelled out by Seg.

"The pigtail fellow Dahram chopped and the woman hired the three thugs to deal with us. Pigtail is dead. Will we ever run across the woman again?"

Dahram boomed. "Aye, doms! She had a nasty mean look about her, did that one."

"All I really saw was that coiled hair and a sharp pointy nose like a witch." As I spoke my gaze probed about among the shadows under the walls where the lights of torches did not reach. "And a ring on her finger the size of a loloo's egg—"

"You exaggerate, dom! As big as a walnut, yes!"

"That'll be a poison ring," said Seg sagely. "She can flip the lid open and pour enough poison into your goblet to shrivel the toes of a regiment of heroes."

"As I remarked," said Dahram the Bold, "a nice class of friends you have." He roared at his own words—a trick some people have that doesn't really offend if you think about them as humans—and then sputtered out: "There's the Calsany and Flea. They hire guards there."

"They sell drinks there," we said together.

Thirsty work, swording.

Although the maniacal wars of the late Empress Thyllis had now ceased, and the civil war was over, there still remained urgent need of fighting men.

The old iron legions of Hamal were being rebuilt. There was still need of mercenaries. Every person, every man woman and child old enough to understand, was aware that the danger from the Fishheads, the Shanks from over the curve of the world, had arrived in full force.

We could only expect this "full force" to become fuller and more powerful in the future.

Dahram the Bold would find a merchant eager enough to hire him.

We settled to our goblets in a quiet corner of the Calsany and Flea.

"Oh, yes, doms," said Dahram, putting his goblet down and wiping the back of his hand across the hair over, below and surrounding his mouth. "I'm from Theakdrin, of which you will never have heard, seeing it is a small kovnate tucked in a bend of the River Os. We were independent for as far back as anyone could remember; then the Hamalese took us over. That was when I was a little shaver. So, I fought for Hamal. Well, it seemed the right thing to do at the time."

"And then?" said Seg.

"Oh, I went for a mercenary. Hyr-paktun. Although you might not believe it—"

"We do."

"In these recent troubles I started off hired out to a kov of Hamal and ended up fighting against him. That's the way it goes in the paktun's trade."

Also, as we saw, though Dahram the Bold might be a hyr-paktun wearing the pakzhan, he had achieved that rare distinction through his own prowess. He was not a leader. He would not control his own band, and hire and fire, seek contracts, conclude deals. He would be in the forefront of the battle, always, earning his hire, fighting with swirling sword, and the pakzhan glittering gold at his throat.

He wanted to know all there was to learn of the black sorcerer and the unholy thaumaturgy that had destroyed the old empress and her followers. We were able to tell him a little of the Wizards of Loh—some of whom are my friends and in no sense black sorcerers—and how the arch-devil had been blown away in a flame of gramarye. He shivered.

"I am a fighting man. Sorcery—no, doms, not for me."

Mere mortals are not allowed the privilege of looking into the future. If it be a privilege, that is. So Dahram the Bold spoke thus, quaffing his ale, with no conception of what fate held in store for him in the way of sorcery. . . .

We were pestered by a Rapa with one arm, whose feathers were mostly bristled off his birdlike face. His beak was dented. He wore rags, and stank.

"Masters—I was once like you—I fought at the Battle of the Incendiary Vosks—masters—an ob, a copper ob, for the sake of Havil the Green—"

Seg threw a few copper obs. The miserable creature scuffled for them. His feathers rustled. He stank.

"I was at that fight," said Dahram, offhandedly.

"Oh?" we said, firing up as your fighting man does at promised reminiscences and soldiers' yarns. "So were we."*

After we decided to leave, Dahram said we were welcome to share his lodgings. A widow woman was most hospitable. We thanked him; but we had our own pads for the night.

So, with the shouted "Remberees!" we parted.

I said, "I must talk to Nedfar about the ex-soldiers. It is cruel that they should be reduced to begging. That Rapa may have stenched worse than a slave-whipmaster's armpit, but he had fought."

Seg has this astonishingly practical turn of mind to set against the fey qualities of his nature. He surprised me yet again.

"Mayhap, Dray And mayhap he had his own arm chopped off and singed his feathers. The rest is mere play-acting."

"Self-mutilation!"

"Successful begging is an art form. It goes in families. You

---

*Here Prescot gives a résumé of the Battle of the Flaming Vosks, fought against the Shanks, and much old-soldier talk is quoted which I am almost sure is parody. A.B.A.

get your trade, you learn it early, you accept your mutilation, and you are set up as a working beggar for life."

"I don't care for that, by Vox!"

But care for it or not, it was true and it went on. We had obliterated all traces of the self-mutilation bit in Vallia; but, for all our careful planning, we still had our beggars. They diminished, season by season; but they were a blot on our so-called civilization.

For some reason I had no desire to retire to bed this early. Sitting at the desk in a small study, part of the luxurious suite of apartments in the Alshyss Tower, I wrote to various people, counseling, inquiring, giving news, occasionally issuing direct orders. I wrote to Djanduin, and Valka, to Zamra and to Veliadrin, to Zenicce and to my wild clansmen of the plains of Segesthes. The burs passed as the water dropped in the clepsydra, and I did not notice. From this small study I could feel in direct contact with all those places in the world of Kregen that are especially dear to me.

I could not, of course, write to Delia.

Where she was, only the Sisters of the Rose knew.

So, and with strokes of the pen rather harder than softer, I directed a letter to Katrin Rashumin in the pious hope she would see that the SoR forwarded it to Delia.

Then I took a fresh sheet of paper, and hesitated.

Drak.

He still was not the Emperor of Vallia.

Finally, I wrote a letter couched in general terms, inquiring particularly after the trouble in the southwest of the island. I also wished to know the progress of our movements in the north and northwest, where Inch and Turko were involved.

Having written to Drak, I could write to my youngest son, Jaidur, who was the King of Hyrklana, and bring him up to date with the news and inquire what went forward in his realms.

And then I went to bed.

The first person I saw the following morning was cheerful old Ortyg ham Hundral, the Pallan of Buildings. He wore a loose round cape and a close-fitting cap they call a havchun. He beamed at me, sipping the hot milk my people had prepared for him.

"Majister! We have discovered the plans of the Temple of Havil in Splendor!"

"This is splendid news, Ortyg," I said, enthused at once.

"We can rebuild houses to fresh patterns; the priests have been insistent that their temples be restored in toto."

We talked on for a space, for the Pallan of the Buildings was a learned man, brought out of retirement. He had had nothing to do with mad Empress Thyllis, living quietly on his estates. He bustled off, cheerfully, and in came Nedfar.

"Please tell me what you propose in respect of the regular regiments of Djangs still in Hamal, Dray. I value them. But some of the people—well, they—"

"They don't like to see foreign troops in their capital city. Well, that is more than understandable."

"It is not quite that. Of course, you are right; but it has more to do with the very ferocity and build of your Djangs."

I laughed.

"My four-armed Djangs will take most foemen apart, yes, I agree. As for your damned stinking Kataki slaver, with his whiptail and bladed steel, Djangs rejoice to blatter Katakis."

"No one likes Katakis."

"They almost took over your country, Nedfar."

"Only through that mad wizard, Phu-Si-Yantong. Well, all that is gone, dust blown with the wind. We admire your Djangs. But we would feel happier if there were apims of Vallia to represent your presence."

"Very good, Nedfar. I'll see to it."

"You had no fortune last night?"

"No." I told Emperor Nedfar what had happened in The Ruby Winespout. "I'm seeing my man today. He has to know more about Spikatur than he has told us so far."

"I could wish the business well away and gone."

"Like your Tyfar and my Jaezila. Is it true that no one knows where they had flown?"

"Perfectly true, for my people. I have asked."

"So have I. When your son and my daughter take it into their heads to plan a little intrigue, all the pressures of Imrien would not pry the secret loose."

"No, by Krun!"

"And," I said, making my voice more courteous, tactful, "the princess Thefi—?"

Nedfar's fierce eyebrows drew down. He had developed as a man wonderfully since he had become emperor, and I was now convinced that the megalomania from which he might easily suffer would be resisted. I'd damned well see to it, if it was not. And, as you will readily perceive, there is the example of my own megalomania. . . .

"My daughter Thefi has been sent to a distant cousin, in the country, to take the fresh air, to recuperate, and to take stock. As for Lobur the Dagger, he is posted at once to a Hamalian Air Service patrol, and is out there over the Mountains of the West fighting the wild men."

"Poor Lobur!"

"And if he can win through, then he may win Thefi. Now, Dray, to business. We must restock the vital arms, we need cavalry mounts, both land and air, we need full-scale production of arrows and varter bolts, we need the mergem process to be speeded up—"

"In short, Nedfar, we need the complete arsenal of a major power in full deployment to beat these confounded Shanks. I agree. So, let us to it!"

Two meal breaks later we surfaced. I said, "I have contracted to go and see Pallan Ortyg ham Hundral. He has found the plans of the Temple of Havil in Splendor—"

Nedfar rubbed a finger along his chin.

"I seem to remember a flying ship of the Djangs dropped buckets of combustibles on that Temple, Dray."

"So I am told. Katakis were shooting varters from it."

In the little ensuing silence we both, in our own ways, regretted the follies and extravagances of battle.

The enormous continent of Havilfar, stretching below the equator, contained many countries and nations, the largest of which was the Empire of Hamal up in the northeast corner. The Kingdom of Djanduin, out in the west, was almost as large. Up above the equator to the north lay the island of Pandahem, divided up into various countries, and divided, also, east to west by a chain of mountains which altered completely the climate of Northern and Southern Pandahem. North of there lay Vallia. . . . And, to the east of Vallia, Valka. . . .

Well, I own it, I sensed the feelings of the people of Hamal. We of Vallia and Valka and Djanduin, with friends from Hyrklana and the Dawn Lands, had rid the world of the mad Empress Thyllis and the arch-fiend, Phu-Si-Yantong. But, well and all, perhaps we'd be better off at home? We might be overstaying our welcome here. I sensed this, in the delicate way Nedfar talked, his graceful gestures, and the way those eyebrows manipulated the shadows over his face.

"We must rebuild Hamal, Nedfar. We must be strong to

face those devilish Shanks who raid us. But I think you know my feelings on having a country fight its own battles."

"Yes," he said wryly. "I remember."

"And I am restless. I am asked this and that, I do this and that, and yet—"

"The Empress Delia?"

"By Zair, how I miss her!"

"Well, my friend, you must go adventuring, as you love so well to do."

"But—"

He smiled, and in his firmness of feature reminded me of his son, Tyfar, who was a blade comrade and who would, if all our friends could knock some sense into him and her, marry my daughter Jaezila.

"Oh, yes, Dray," said the Emperor of Hamal, "there are always buts."

Then Seg came in after knocking and I was able to dissimulate. By Krun! But Nedfar was right!

"Seg!" I said, and I spoke so that my comrade swung instantly to face me, and I saw that quickly suppressed flick of his hand, ready to draw sword or bow. "Seg, my old dom. You and I are due for some roving again—we have nothing now to detain us here."

"That is true. I have the Kroveres of Iztar, but we are busily recruiting and things go passably well—"

"We will visit Vallia and Valka—"

"Visit?"

Nedfar saw what Seg meant.

"Can you visit your home?"

For me, an Earthman transited across four hundred light-years of emptiness to a marvelous and wonderful new world—to such a one—where did home lie? With Delia, yes. But she was off adventuring, driven by compulsions a mere mortal man was not allowed to share. Home? Yes, Valka was my home, up there in the high fortress castle of Esser Rarioch overlooking Valkanium and the bay. And, too, the gorgeous enclave city of Zenicce was home to me. and so were the tents of my ferocious Clansmen of Segesthes. And, too, so was the windy city of Djanguraj in my Kingdom of Djanduin. I have many homes, many I have not spoken of. But I think in the end a fellow's true home is what he carries in his head. Where his thoughts lie, that is home.

Another knock sounded and the two guards opened the doors with a quick check of the fellow they admitted.

Protocol, at least for the Emperor of Vallia, was deliberately relaxed.

One of the guards, old whiskery Rubin who could sink a stoup of ale without pause and who had been in one or another of my regiments for a long long time, opened his mouth and bellowed: "Majister! Andoth Hardle, the Spy, craves audience!"

I did not burst out laughing. But, by Vox, I own my craggy old beakhead split into a most ferocious smile of pleasure. Good old Rubin. Spies, like anyone else, had to be announced to the emperor unless they were personal friends.

"He," observed Seg, "won't be a spy for long if Rubin shouts any louder."

"Send him in, Rubin," I said.

"Quidang!"

And so my latest spy, Andoth Hardle, trotted in.

Trotted. Well, he was small and lithe and wore a chin beard, and was deft and inconspicuous, quick with a dagger, and wearing link mesh under his tunic. He bowed.

"Majister."

"Sit down, Andoth, and take a glass. Your news?"

"The woman with the coiled hair has been taken up."

"What!" exclaimed Seg. "So easily?"

Andoth Hardle sat in the chair that did not stand next to my desk, and he delicately filled the glass on the side table with parclear. He put the jug down and rearranged the linen cover. He lifted the glass and the parclear sparkled.

One does not ordinarily toast in parclear.

"Taken up, Kov Seg. She was discovered lying in the gutter, drunk and stupid."

At once Seg and I believed we understood.

"Poor soul," said Seg, and he spoke softly.

Nedfar, too, caught the drift.

"Yet, she was an enemy, and would have destroyed us."

"True."

"You will see her, majister?" Hardle drank and wiped his lips daintily with lace-trimmed linen from his sleeve.

"I will see her, Andoth."

Seg looked in my direction, and I nodded. Of course.

Then I said, "Andoth. This is good news. But, before I see her, make sure she is sober and cleaned up, given fresh clothes if necessary, fed and cared for."

"I understand, majister. It shall be as you command."

"Does she give a name?"

Hardle twisted his head sideways. "She is not, majister, the Lady Helvia. At least, she says her name is Pancresta."

"I see. Send for Hamdi the Yenakker. Have him study this woman, and do not let her see him. I feel there is a great deal we can learn from her."

So that was how it was arranged. But privately I wondered just how much we would ever learn about Spikatur Hunting Sword.

Chapter Three

Questions for Spikatur

The corridors, sculpted from rock, trimmed with rock, arched and groined with rock, loomed grim and forbidding. The walls ran with moisture. Torches hurled sharp sparks from glittering particles embedded in the walls. The floor slimed slippery underfoot. These were dungeons.

Yet the woman Pancresta had been placed in a room furnished with some comfort, with carpets and wall hangings, with tables and chairs, and a brazier against the underground damp and chill. Her room would not have shamed a middle-class hotel.

She stood up as we entered.

Her coiled hair was neatly arranged. She wore a long blue robe, and the hems were trimmed with fur. A cheap fur, perhaps, but soft and warm. Her face was pale.

While that was natural, the paleness was more a habitual absence of high color than a result of her capture, her present predicament. This, I felt strongly.

Her face was of the long, plain, strong type, with prominent cheekbones, and a tight mouth. She had worn armor, and a sword belted around those lean hips. She would be mean in a fight, and mean elsewhere, and now she was filled with a vindictive desire to revenge herself for the death of her lover.

I said, "Mistress Pancresta?"

She inclined that hard face, and the coiled hair caught the light.

"You will not believe me, Mistress Pancresta, if I express sorrow for the deaths of your companions. But it is so. Needless death offends me."

"Death is not needless when it is such as you who should die."

30

Seg opened his mouth, and I said, and I think I surprised her, "Why?"

"Why?"

She opened her eyes fully. They were dark with pain.

"Yes. Why is it needful that I die?"

"Because you are one of the lordly ones."

I laughed.

"I? A lordly one? You mock me, Mistress Pancresta."

Her hard face did not flush; but her lips tightened still more.

She fairly spat out: "You are the Emperor of Vallia. That, alone, marks you for destruction."

"As to that," I said casually, "I'm inclined to agree with you. But that has nothing to do with death."

She was puzzled.

"You speak in riddles."

"No. I speak in words that will be understood by those who have the intelligence to understand."

"Now you mock me."

Truth to tell, true though all this was, it was of small comfort to me, knowing that I intended to shift the job of being Emperor of Vallia off onto my fine son Drak. Still; he was born to be an emperor. I had merely gained that job by my sword and by election. There were differences. And, mind you, my way may very well be the better of the two. . . .

"I would like you to tell me what you know of Spikatur Hunting Sword."

She smiled then, a hard and cruel smile. But I fancied there was uncertainty in it, too.

"Spikatur will sweep you and all your kind away."

"You mean you will go around murdering all the people you don't like?"

"No—it is not like that—"

"Then what is it like?"

"It is a Great Jikai!"*

I frowned. The misuse of the word jikai does not amuse me.

"I allow there are many princes and kings in this world who would be better off out of it. But not all. And not all the

*Jikai: this word here quite clearly carries the meaning of Crusade. A.B.A.

ordinary folk you people murder. You are drenched in blood, and most of it is blood of innocent people."

Now, Nedfar was a man of high principles, a man of impeccable integrity, as I knew. He had been talked to long and long before agreeing to become the Emperor of Hamal. But, for all that, he was a natural-born prince, a Prince of Kregen. Now he coughed a dry little cough and spoke firmly. "I am against the use of torture. It dismays and sickens me. But in certain cases—"

Seg said, "Careful, Emperor. Dray is sensitive on that point."

Nedfar's reply was brusque.

"So am I, Kov Seg. But my good friend Trylon Agrival was foully murdered the other week by these monsters. He was a man steeped in the ancient lore of the Sunset People. Why should they murder him?"

"Because," burst out the woman, "he pried into secrets we were never meant to discover."

Extraordinarily difficult, by Krun, to argue against beliefs of this kind!

But argue one must. At least, argue and talk and cajole. Torture—no. I'd have no part of that, and neither would Seg. And, while my regiments remained in Hamal, neither would Nedfar, comrade or no. And there spoke the voice of paranoia, loud and clear. . . .

I said, "I have struggled against unjust authority all my life. I have been slave. I have been whipped and tortured and chained in far fouler dungeons than any you may imagine, Mistress Pancresta. I do understand so much of what Spikatur Hunting Sword originally stood for." I used the Spikatur oath. "By Sasco! I have fought alongside the adherents of Spikatur!"

She looked surprised not so much at what I said, for that could all be a hollow shell of lies, designed to trick her, but at my use of the oath calling on Sasco.

"What do you know, fool, of Spikatur?"

So I told her what little we knew. The Spikatur Hunting Sword conspiracy had begun as a force to defeat Hamal. We believed it originated in Pandahem. It was made up of groups of people and owned no single leader..

At this she leered at me, and her voice thickened.

"This is all over now."

Seg whistled.

I saw what she had let slip.

She, too, saw. Her lids lowered over her eyes. Her mouth clamped to a bar.

"We shall leave now, Mistress Pancresta. But we shall return. I need answers to those questions. If you know, I think it would be wise to answer."

"We of Spikatur Hunting Sword are not afraid to die for what we believe."

"I know," I said, and we went out and left her alone.

And then Nedfar, regal, dazzling in his robes, a prince, the Emperor of Hamal, turned at the door as the guards prepared to clang the bars shut.

"Remember, Mistress Pancresta. Dying is easy. It is of the manner of dying that you should think."

Seg started to say as we walked up that dolorous corridor: "You wouldn't really—"

Nedfar shook his head.

"Of course not. But dark thoughts loosen tongues."

The whole scene here distressed me, because a woman was incarcerated, because we were trying to force her to reveal what she had sworn to keep hidden, because the naked face of force was being used. But remembering old Trylon Agrival did make the point. He had been a Vallian, visiting Hamal and seeking to uncover the riddles of the past. He was gentle, absorbed in his work, a man out of the run of politics. Nedfar and Agrival had struck up a firm friendship. Agrival had tended to wander off into ruins, poking and prying, trying to read the old inscriptions. Such a man was very far from the lordly ones of Kregen, rubbing the noses of the poor in the dirt.

Yet the assassins of Spikatur Hunting Sword had murdered him.

I felt that a new wave of terror would be unleashed, that this new leader the Spikatur adherents had acquired, this dark unknown, would bring down all that we had been struggling to achieve.

Once, I had seen Spikatur as a potent if suspect weapon in the struggle against Hamal. Now that weapon was being turned against the very people who had emerged successfully from the fight against Hamal—the Hamal represented by mad Empress Thyllis—and against innocent people who stood aloof from the conflict. This did make sense. But in the context of Kregen and the future we all faced in dealing with the marauding Shanks, the sense was completely overshadowed by the greater sense of mutual preservation and freedom.

"Cheer up, my old dom," quoth Seg as we emerged into the glorious twinned rays of the Suns of Scorpio. "Now this fresh air after those dungeons gives me an appetite."

"Capital," I said, and off we went to find our second breakfast.

Not in the mood for one of those huge festive meals of Kregen, Seg and I bade a temporary farewell to Nedfar and took ourselves off to our private rooms. There we ate well, quaffed good Kregen tea, and discussed just what we planned to do.

As usual, Seg took up the latest stave on which he was practicing his magic. In due time that stave would become a superb bowstave. There is, as I have said before and will no doubt say again, no finger archer in all Kregen than Seg Segutorio. His face was intent as he worked.

"And you plan to take off, leave all this high life, tramp off into the wilderness?"

"If fate takes me that way. Otherwise, I plan a little jaunt to a few places I know where one may come by some action, a few drinks, good food and a lot of laughs—"

"You will go alone?"

"Only if you elect not to come."

He looked up quickly, and the fey blueness of his eyes struck like daggered lightning through a black overcast. He smiled. He gave the stave a tremendous buffet so that it spun around and around.

"The elections have just taken place," he said.

So that was all right.

Then whiskery Rubin stuck his head around the door and bellowed.

Rubin, incidentally, like so many of my old swods, was a Zan Deldar and would, at his own request, remain so. Not for him the escalation of the dizzy heights. He could become a Hikdar, the next rank up, at once, should he so wish. It would not be long before he was a Jiktar. It would take a little longer, a matter of a decade, if no one got massacred too recklessly, before he made Chuktar. But for whiskery Rubin, being a Deldar, and a Zan Deldar, the top of the tree, at that, was ambition, reward and pleasure enough.

"Majister! Hamdi the Yenakker craves audience."

"Show him in, Rubin, please." I glanced across sharply. "You have been on duty a long time."

"Aye, majister. Standing in for young Long Wil, who has a twisted shoulder."

"Oh?"

Rubin looked evasive. The magnificence of his uniform was entirely superficial. All the gold and braids and feathers would not interfere with his sword arm. But he did look splendid. His medals—the bobs—on his chest glittered.

"Fell, majister, twisted his shoulder."

Far be it from me to inquire further. But, just to be devilish and to let my swods know I wasn't senile yet, I walked across, digging out a gold zan-deldy piece. This I placed in the horny palm of Rubin.

"Puggled, winner or loser. You will know, Zan Deldar Rubin, who deserves this acknowledgment from me."

"Aye, majister, may the glory of Opaz shine on us all."

He stiffened up into attention. On Kregen it could not be ramrod attention; but he stiffened up as straight as one of Seg's best shafts. His face, brown and lined and like a chunk of that hard stone they can never seem to break under a year's hard labor in distant Shalasfreel, betrayed nothing. If Long Wil had been in a fight, his comrades would see to it that the deserving of the combatants received the gold. And ten gold pieces, in one zan-deldy coin, was a matter of consideration. I did not think Long Wil had fallen down drunk. That behavior tended to exclude folk from the ranks of my various guard units.

As Hamdi the Yenakker sidled in I reflected that this little aside with Rubin was not unimportant. Of little incidents like this was the trust between commander and men forged, for there was nothing here of the insulting patronage of handing out money as largesse without reason beyond the buying of men's loyalty. My men and I swore our mutual loyalties by the edge of the sword.

"Well, Hamdi?"

"Majister. She is the woman I warned you of."

"So I gathered. This Pancresta. Sit down and take a glass. What else have you learned?"

"She is from Pandahem. From south. I do not trust her. But she asks for an audience with you, majister."

"Does she? Well, Hamdi, you rogue, as you well know I do not trust you. Oh, we have done business in the past. But mayhap this time. . . . Who knows?"

Hamdi looked hurt. He was still the same tall and up-right fellow, carrying himself with a swagger, now sworn to all things Vallian after our victory over mad Empress Thyllis. But he understood we knew he was a rogue. I feel that upset him only in that he felt less free to practice his wiles. Well, nothing much need be said about Hamdi the Yenakker. He sold us information. He provided contacts. He had his uses.

And, so far, he had not betrayed us.

"Have I not served you well, majister? Was it not I who took you and Kov Seg here to The Crushed Toad to meet Nath the Dwa? Have I not provided you with trustworthy information? Did I not save the life of young Strom Nomius?"

"Aye, Hamdi, you did warn us in time to prevent his assassination. But to the matter of the woman—"

"Yes, majister. I think she wishes to trick you by giving you false information." He stood up for himself. "Unlike me."

Seg said, "I could wish Deb-Lu or Khe-Hi were here."

"Aye."

Had our two comrades who were Wizards of Loh been available on hand, they might well have riddled out if Pancresta spoke the truth. As it was, the Wizards were about their own business.

Then Hamdi said, "Has—pressure—been exerted on the woman, majister?"

"No," I said. His look was sly, understanding, a tilt to his head and a sidelong glance conveying what he was hinting at. "Nothing like that, and nothing like that will be permitted while Kov Seg or myself remain in command."

"Well, majister, something made her wish to talk."

I would not open out on a speculation on the results of Nedfar's threat. I said, "It is probably as you say. She wishes to trick us. I will see her."

Hamdi screwed up his eyes.

"There is one thing—"

"Yes?"

"—She insists that she meet you privately, in the open, away from spying eyes."

Carefully, Seg said, "Can she insist?"

"She was, kov, most insistent."

"She must be afraid of others of Spikatur. If she sells them, they will surely seek to kill her."

"That is right," I said. "But it suggests there are loopholes in the security here."

"It is all Hamalese, now, apart from this wing of the palace."

"All right." One woman, alone, deserved her fair chance of life. "I'll see her as she wishes."

"I shall arrange it, majister."

Hamdi rose, finishing his glass of parclear, and bowed. I let him. He put store by these things. When he had gone, Seg said, "All right, Dray. So you meet her and some hidden stikitche puts a shaft through your back."

"So I shall wear a breast and back."

"If it was me, I'd put one through whatever of you was unarmored. That'd be your vosk-skull of a head."

"Most assassins are not as good shots as you."

"Any stikitche worth contracting could hit your head."

The point of this wrangle was perfectly clear. Seg wanted to come along, too. I did not say him nay.

There was time to see Ortyg ham Hundral, Pallan of Buildings, and to join with him in gleeful contemplation of the plans of the Temple of Havil in Splendor. I had only one fleeting thought at the oddness of this. Not so long ago I'd have been straining every nerve to destroy every damned temple erected to Havil the Green.

Times change, by Zair!

When Hamdi the Yenakker reported back the location chosen for the meeting with Pancresta, I own to an odd feeling of the rightness of the choice.

The bloodiness of the Arena in Ruathytu was notorious throughout the length and breadth of the continent of Havilfar. I had not fought there at that time, although the ways of the Star Lords are passing strange and beyond the full comprehension of mortal men; but I had fought in the Arena of Huringa in Hyrklana. Along with many others, I had set my face against the idea of the Jikhorkdun, the Arena, the killing machinery of deadly games on the silver sand.

In the Great Arena, here in Ruathytu, the arch devil Phu-Si-Yantong, that infamous Wizard of Loh, had made his last stand, his final resistance, until blown away in the Quern of Gramarye fashioned by our comrade Wizards of Loh.

Since that awful occurrence, the place had not been popular, we had done all we could to discourage attendance, and the other smaller Jikhorkdums had reopened to patronage we deplored. So the Great Arena lay deserted under the Suns, and the silver sand sparkled unmarked by the tramp of booted feet, the rush of talons, the sprinkle of shed blood.

Here, out on the silver sand, Pancresta chose to meet us and tell us the secrets of Spikatur Hunting Sword.

Chapter Four

What Chanced in the Arena

The Emperor of Hamal said in his sternest voice, "Remember, Dray Prescot, you are the Emperor of Vallia. And King of Djanduin. And many other notable titles and ranks. It is not fitting that you should not go attired as an emperor."

"As to that," I said, adjusting the plain lesten hide belt with the silver buckle, "I never feel comfortable in all that popinjay finery."

Seg let loose a cross between a grunt and a chuckle.

So, quickly, very quickly, I said, "I speak only for myself, Nedfar. You, I am sure, understand that."

Nedfar took it in good part.

He was dressed magnificently, a shimmering statuesque emperor, a lordly one of Kregen, dominating and superb.

Seg and I wore the brave old scarlet, with a cunning coat of mesh-linked mail, and over that we wore a breast and back apiece, since that pleased Seg on my behalf. Our harness was plain, workmanlike, without any of your frills. The smell of rich leather-oil pervaded the chamber not unpleasantly. I say rich—any fighting man will use the best equipment he can lay his hands on, and taking care of weapons and harness is a number-one priority. That oil was expensive.

Seg found himself in something of a quandary.

His strong face loooked puzzled. I laughed and said, "Luckily enough I am not in that predicament."

He hefted two bows, one in each hand, and he looked at and weighed one and then he looked at and weighed the other.

Finally, he said, "Were it not thought excessive, what our old comrade Fran the Zappim would call Vulgar Ostentation, I would take them both."

39

"Even a Djang finds difficulty in shooting two bows at once. They do not recommend the practice, and—"

"And they have four arms! I know. . . ."

"We are only going to speak to a poor woman, alone, out on the silver sand."

"I don't trust her."

"No more do I. Take them both, then. They will snug up over your shoulder well enough, seeing they are so alike."

He made that little grunting chuckle of his, and shook his head, and shoved both bowstaves up over his shoulder.

"I may look a ninny, but that does not bother me."

Nedfar shared the general amusement over Seg and his precious bows.

We strapped up our usual arsenal of weaponry—a rapier and main gauche, a drexer, a shoulder pack of throwing knives, those little deadly weapons the girls of the great clans of Segesthes call the Deldar, a hunting knife, odds and ends of lethal nastiness. Weight had to figure into all this, of course, but a fellow can carry a tremendous load when his life depends on it, and we took nothing we felt we did not need or might not require.

For helmets, which we took because Nedfar insisted, we chose plain, smoothly round, headpieces, rather like basinets, and the gallant red feathers flaunted from minuscule silver rosettes. Over all we each flung a scarlet cape. This was, perhaps, carrying effect to extremes; but I had taken some heed of Nedfar's words.

So dressed up in a curious mixture of men going off to war and men intending merely to impress, we set off.

If I do not mention that snugly scabbarded down my back lay a Krozair longsword, it is merely because whenever the opportunity offers I take a specimen of that great brand as a matter of course. There was, I firmly believed, on Kregen only one pattern of sword superior to the Krozair longsword, and that was the marvelous Savanti sword.

So, dressed and accoutred and with a good meal under our belts, we went down to the courtyard and mounted our zorcas.

As we rode along through the crowded streets after the short haul across the river, our zorcas patient of this delay before we remounted, I reflected on how well I knew this once-hostile city, how great and magnificent a place it was, and yet how different in atmosphere from the other great cities I knew on Kregen.

Everywhere people were busy about the task of rehabilitation. The place hummed with activity. Our small bodyguard rode at our backs, a party of Nedfar's personal guards, and a half-dozen files of my duty squadron, which happened to be this day from IESW. The First Regiment of the Emperor's Sword Watch. I knew every man, and every man knew me. But, as we rode, we attracted little attention.

For this I was glad, but it showed all too clearly that the people of Ruathytu might have misinterpreted the attitude of their new emperor.

Nedfar rode between us, and presently he half-leaned sideways and said to me, "The Empress Thyllis would never have ridden through her capital city like this, Dray. There would have been processions, and regiments of guards, and chanting and singing everywhere she went."

I acknowledged the truth of this observation.

"The people do not fawn on me, and that is good. It seems your brand of emperorship works here in Hamal as well as in your Vallia."

"That pleases me. I can't stand the sight of rows of upturned bottoms."

Seg laughed.

The sounds and scents of a busy city surrounded us. But as we neared the Jikhorkdun the clamor fell away. The aqueducts bulked black against the sky. The cobbles rang louder under the hooves of the zorcas. These splendid riding animals, proud, curvetting, each with his single spiral horn jutting arrogantly from his forehead, were full of fire and mettle.

And the Arena brooded like a dark blot upon the city.

Hamdi the Yenakker waited for us inside the first of the shadows.

He bowed most respectfully to Nedfar.

"Lahal, Emperor!"

Nedfar acknowledged with a Lahal and a gesture, and then we dismounted and, with the guards closed up around us, went through the first of the warren of courtyards and practice rings and bazaars. Everywhere they lay deserted and empty.

Once this place would have been frantic with the every day carryings-on of the Jikhorkdun. The booths were shuttered, the stalls empty. The practice rings gaped blindly.

Through the colossal arches supporting the seating of the amphitheater we went, and our booted feet rang hollow echoes.

And so we stepped out from one of the ring of gateways, out onto the sands of the Arena, out onto the Silver Sand.

One could fancy all those rows and rows of seats, towering up into the sky, filled with the insensate beast-roar of a blood-mad crowd. Thousands of people, screaming with the blood lust upon them, and, down here where we stood, a small forlorn group, the kaidurs would have fought and died.

I gave a little shivery shake of my shoulders.

An airboat drifted in over the stands, lowering down to the sand.

Seg said, "At least she travels in comfort."

"It was thought best, kov, by the Jiktar of the guard." Hamdi spread his hands, saying it was no affair of his. The airboat settled out in the center of the arena.

Nedfar took a step forward.

He halted, and turned to us.

I do not see why—at that stage—we felt tense, jumpy. We were just humoring a proud and willful woman, attempting to gain secrets from her without the use of force. But, all the same, I own to putting my fist down onto the hilt of my drexer, and of looking sharply into the blue-black shadows around the arena.

"Dray?" said Nedfar.

"You are emperor here now, Nedfar."

"Only because of you. . . . Very well. Let us all go out together."

Seg, Nedfar and I walked across the silver sand.

Sometimes, in the old days, the Jikhorkdun of Ruathytu had used golden sand.

Red blood still looked dark and unwholesome, spilt on gold as on silver sand.

The heat beat down. The suns were halfway down, sending mingled shadows across the floor of the arena. All the rows of flagstaffs were bare of treshes, naked and like withered sticks after a gale.

Pancresta alighted from the airboat.

We walked on.

She advanced to meet us.

We would meet just over halfway.

She wore her long blue gown, open now at the throat. Even at this distance she gave the impression of hard dominance, of authority, of determination. She walked well.

"We have done well," said Nedfar, "to have caged this one."

"Aye," said Seg.

The way Nedfar observed that we had done well, and my own observation that Pancresta walked well, chimed. One supported the other. The Arena in Ruathytu is large. We took our time walking to this meeting. All the time we strode on, in a strange and affecting way, yet in no sense a weird or eerie way, I could hear the crazed roar of a blood-lusting crowd in my head. I could hear them, and if I half-closed my eyes I could see them—see the rows of inflamed faces and upraised fists, see the spectators as I fought out on the Silver Sand, see them all, by Beng Thrax's Glass Eye and Brass Sword!

In the airboat parked beyond the advancing form of Pancresta the guards waited. There were not many of them in the small flier; after all, they merely guarded a lone woman. They were Hamalese, decked out in blue and green and with a deal of silver lace and colored feathers.

An airboat flitted in over the western edge of the amphitheatre. Seg glanced up, following my gaze.

Nedfar said, "I gave orders that the patrols should be active."

By the way we walked, the way we talked and, I suppose, by the way we thought, we gave an enormous importance to this woman Pancresta. Incongruous? I was beginning to think so when the airboat abruptly swooped.

She passed directly over the flier that had brought the woman to this meeting.

A small dark object tumbled out, and then another and another.

They dropped down, plummeting into the flier.

They were not pots of combustibles.

"What?" said Nedfar, and he halted.

A man leaped from the parked flier.

He flailed his arms around his head. He danced like a crazy man. Another followed him, and then a third. They swirled and beat their arms. Around their heads a hazy shadow drifted, joining and parting, a greyish shroud lapping them together in a cloud of torment.

"Wasps," said Seg. "Or bees."

"Aye."

We started to run. Seg and I raced over the silver sands, and as we ran so we drew our swords.

No thought of the incongruousness of all this armory could

stand now against the stark reality of the trick by which we
had been fooled.

Pancresta stopped. She looked up. She held up her arms.

There was tremendous triumph in the gesture.

The voller sweeping through the air dived low, flew above
her and a net spun out, a mesh of glinting silver.

The net grasped Pancresta as she grasped the strands.

In a twinkling she was drawn up.

She vanished over the coaming of the voller and the airboat pivoted, rose and stormed away. She disappeared over
the lip of the amphitheatre.

The whole thing was over in the time a rapier takes to
pierce a man's lung.

Seg stuffed his sword back into the scabbard and I did the
same. There was no need for us to exchange words.

Both of us knew what had happened.

We belted in a straight run for the abandoned flier.

Corruption had been at work, bribery, force. The
Hamalese guards had been got at. Pancresta's friends had
been in communication with her in her dungeon cell. A
guard had acted as a go-between. The chances were strong
that he was himself a secret member of Spikatur Hunting
Sword. Whatever the truth of that, the result was plain. The
patrol had been outwitted, a flier had snatched up the
woman, and the guards were reeling about, screaming, stung
and bitten and tormented.

Seg and I bundled into the voller.

She went up with Seg at the controls like a stone from a
catapult.

Low Seg hurled her, low over the topmost tier of seating.
We scraped across and shot away.

"There," said Seg.

Ahead of us, speeding into the sunset fires of red and jade,
the dark shape of the voller flitted like a moth against a lan-
tern.

As we watched she turned northward, swinging in a wide
arc.

Instantly, Seg swung the levers of the craft over and we
hared off to cut the corner.

"We won't lose them now," I said.

"They have a fast airboat. It will be a long chase."

"Aye."

Below us, glimpsed and lost as we sped on, the smoking

wreckage of a guard voller appeared and disappeared. She had obviously been burned by Pancresta's friends.

"Just put your foot down to your left, will you, my old dom?"

I glanced down and then did as Seg requested.

The crunch did not please me.

"I'll check if there are any more—"

A few more half-drunken wasps were disposed of.

The strange thing—and I make a particular note of the strangeness of it—was my complete lack of emotion when I saw the brown and red scorpion. He waddled out from under a fold of a flying fur. I just squashed him.

I was so wrought up with mortification at the simple way Pancresta had tricked us, I just did not have time to dwell on the propensities of the Star Lords for sending scorpions to whisk me off to other parts of Kregen, or to send me packing home to Earth, four hundred light-years away.

And, anyway—home?

My home was on Kregen.

Seg said, "Cleansing finished?"

"As far as I can see. Do we keep up with them?"

"Just. The vollers are well matched."

I glanced back over the stern.

"There is no one following us."

"Ha," said Seg. "We did get away smartish."

"Yes."

We were two old campaigners and we worked together as a team. We did not waste words, unless we jested. I know Seg was as affronted as I that we had been so easily sucked in.

Even in the rush of wind the voller held the tang of spilled wine. The Hamalese guards had started their drinking early. I found a simple earthenware jug that might contain ale or water or oil, and prised the stopper out and sniffed.

"A middling Stuvan, Seg. You will join me?"

"The Spikatur rascals used pots of stinging insects and scorpions. They did not, I fancy, poison the wine. Yes, my old dom, I will join you."

As I poured I reflected that the Spikatur people had been clever. They had burned a guard voller outside the Jikhorkdun. They had dropped their little stinging allies on the airboat inside the arena. No doubt the guards were rushing to the burning flier, and Nedfar was having some difficulty in finding guards and fliers to obey his orders inside the amphitheatre. Had they burned the voller that had brought Pancresta, the

flier in which we now pursued them, they'd have been
swamped by patrols.

As it was, Seg and I were just two people to chase them
out of all the patrolling guards.

Ironic.

Yet for me, and I thought for Seg, also, this was just what
the doctor ordered, as they used to say.

There exist on Kregen as well as Earth bone-dry pundits
who scorn tales of adventure. If these people lack the breadth
of imagination to encompass an understanding of the
pressures on, condition of, illumination of and triumphs and
failures of the human spirit then that is their loss, not ours.
The unwillingness to accept defeat tamely does not brand a
person as a monster—it may, of course. But then, that is
what adventure tends to do, sort the sheep from the goats, the
ponshos from the leems, make people face themselves, shorn
of pretensions, and—perhaps, if they are lucky—grasp at a
little of what the human spirit exists at all for. . . .

Seg and I were off, and we were off on adventure-bent, and
Spikatur was only half the answer and hardly any of the reason.

Chapter Five

The Hissing of the Star Lords' Chair

How terrible to live in a world without color!

Or, rather, given the universal prodigality of Nature's palette, a world in which you could not see and appreciate color. To live in a monochrome world. . . .

The sheeting lights, rippling and undulating across the sky, the streaming mingled radiance of the Suns of Scorpio, jade and ruby, illuminating everything in fires of crimson and emerald—nothing. You'd see nothing of this in a world without color. . . .

You'd see a pale ghost rising in the sky as the first of Kregen's seven Moons, The Maiden with the Many Smiles, lifted over the horizon. Her pinkish radiance flooded down, adding to the lighting of the world. Soon she was joined by her sister, She of the Veils, whose more mellow golden and rose light mingled and softened the pinkness. The surface of Kregen wallowed in color and light.

And, high through the air, the two vollers bore on.

"We just keep pace," observed Seg.

"The suns will soon be gone—"

"Aye. But we have moons for the whole of tonight."

Not for a single mur this night would real darkness fall. On some nights when not a moon shines in Kregen's sky folk say that it is a Night of Notor Zan. And when all seven moons form their intricate dances into a single configuration of brightness, a line of radiance, folk say that it is the Scarf of Our Lady Monafeyom.

No moon would be at the full tonight, and so Our Lady Monafeyom's Scarf would not be seen.

But there would be ample light for us to track and follow the fleeing airboat.

Like a flitting black bat she darted ahead, fleeting, wispy, a phantom under the Moons of Kregen.

47

Seg and I took watch and watch, turn and turn about.

We flew North.

The land of Hamal passed away below.

In the small hours the wine ran out.

Seg said, "Soup?"

"I'm with you, Seg."

The Hamalese guards had provided themselves with rations, not being entirely stupid, and in the Kregan way taking care that they were victualled against a long spell of duty. Seg brought out the crockery pot of soup, and undid its linen cover. He shook the pot and sniffed.

"Vosk and Taylyne—"

"Excellent."

Now we were used to drinking this soup hot, whereas many Hamalese drank it cold. We were flying up north toward the equator, and although fairly high in the air, and at night, we were not too cold. All the same, Vosk and Taylyne soup is, in our opinion, best drunk hot.

Taylynes are pea-sized vegetables, scarlet and orange, and they blend with Vosk, which is one of the most succulent meats of all Kregen, to form a truly splendid soup.

Seg found the slate slab and the box of combustibles and then fished around in his pouch and brought out his tinder box.

Fire may be produced by many different methods, on Kregen as on Earth, and the tinder box Seg happened to have was one of those little devices the Kregans call januls. He struck flint and steel with unthinking skill, and the tinder caught and flared. In no time the combustible box perched on its slate slab was chucking out the heat.

The soup pot went onto the holder, and Seg sat back, rubbing his hands.

"Any bread?"

He rummaged around in the linen bag and came up with a squat, round, flat, brown loaf.

He sniffed.

"It is leavened, but only just."

"Munsha bread, from one of those shops along Baker's Alley, I'll be bound. Well, it may not be done in the bols style; it will go down a treat."

"Aye."

The soup began to warm up.

We had covered the forward angles with a flap of cloth, both to protect the combustible box from the slipstream and to conceal the glow. A narrow chink of light escaped aft where the box was beginning to corrode and break down.

The shaft of light, smoky orange, fell on the deck.

It glinted from the chape of a sword scabbard, and threw the grain of the wooden deck into relief. I sniffed the aroma of the soup, as Seg broke the bread and looked for butter.

Into that narrow bar of smoky light waddled a scorpion.

"I thought," I said in some disgust, "I'd cleared all the dratted things away."

Seg took no notice.

He sat, half-bent, and the yellow butter on his knife remained unmoving just above the munsha bread.

I stared.

"Seg!"

The scorpion waddled forward.

He was russet and black, banded in glisten, and his sting curved up over his back, arrogantly.

I threw a frantic glance at the controls.

The levers were hooked up with their ropes onto a straight northerly course so that we could prepare our meal and eat in comfort. The voller would fly on. I stared back at the scorpion. He halted on the edge of that narrow band of orange light, glaring at me.

I felt sick.

I knew that my foot could not crush this scorpion.

He waved his sting over his back.

"Dray Prescot," the scorpion said to me, "you are summoned to an audience of the Everoinye."

I swallowed.

At least, this was new.

The Everoinye—the Star Lords—actually telling me they wanted to see me! Damned odd. Frightening, too, for usually the Star Lords just sent their damned scorpion, or their equally damned but hugely large blue Scorpion, and whisked me off.

I said, "Scorpion?"

"You are ready?"

I took a breath.

"You mock me, you must do so."

"Perhaps. It is not for you to inquire into my—"

"Save it, you miniature monster, save it. I know all about my own ineptness and stupidity and how I must not pry into things far beyond my intelligence."

The stinger curled and uncurled.

If that showed the scorpion's anger I did not know or care.

"Get on with it, scorpion. Summon your big blue brother. Let's get this thing over and done with."

And, all the time, Seg remained frozen. He poised, static, and the yellow butter slicked on the knife.

That splendid yellow color took on an unhealthy green tinge. The world turned blue. Blue radiance fell about me.

Waiting for the cold, and the rushing wind, and the endless fall into emptiness, my main emotion was one of irritation. This surprised me. Oh, yes, there was fear in there. I was scared practically witless.

These unknowable people, the Star Lords, possessed awful powers. I was well aware of that. They could hurl me about Kregen, naked and weaponless, to fight for them. They could more dreadfully contemptuously fling me back to Earth, where I was born, four hundred light-years away. They could ruin my life—again.

I waited as the blue radiance dropped about me and the leering form of a giant Scorpion reared above me.

Irritated.

That was it. Through all my panic, irritation with the interruption to my own plans was my main feeling.

Deuced odd.

Usually I was mad clean through, filled with anger, roaring and raging against the Everoinye and their Scorpion, or their messenger and spy, the gorgeous bird, the Gdoinye, in his scarlet and golden feathers. As it was, I just felt like hurling my hat to the deck and jumping on it.

The blueness brightened and cleared. The cold ceased. The fall ended.

I stood on a crimson tiled floor. Crimson walls curved up all about me, arching overhead into a crimson vault in which the brilliant white glitter of stars formed constellations unknown to me.

This chamber, I thought, I had visited before.

I tried to swallow and my mouth was as dry as a pauper's tankard.

The voice whispered in from nowhere and everywhere.

"Sit in the chair, Dray Prescot. Sit."

I licked my lips.

"What damned chair—?" I started to bluster.

The chair sizzled out of the enveloping crimson. It rushed toward me like a runaway totrix, flapping draperies, rippling fringes, lurched to a halt touching my knees. I twisted and fell into the seat. The arms reared up and lapped across my chest like the tentacles of an octopus and the chair hared off, hissing, racing away into the crimson shadows.

This was not madness.

No draught animals pulled the chair. It just went howling along across the floor, hissing, and when it careered around an invisible corner neither it nor I leaned over.

Expecting the light to turn from crimson to green and then to yellow, and to finish up in an ebon chamber with three oval pictures on the walls, I did not close my eyes.

No shimmering veils of gossamer brushed my cheeks.

Pungent scents stung my nostrils.

My eyes watered.

My nose ran.

I tried to clean myself up and the straps held my arms fast locked.

So, then, irritated beyond measure, I yelled.

"Everoinye! Star Lords! What footling nonsense is this?"

They heard me all right. I did not doubt that.

But they did not deign to reply.

After a space I gave up raging at them and calling them all the foul names I could put tongue to, and sat in a dull stupor waiting for what nonsense they would bring on next.

Abruptly, the chair stopped.

There was no sudden jolt. My insides did not give a forward lurch as we halted. One moment we were spinning along, the next we stopped. The transition, abrupt, made no difference to my posture or feelings.

The chair hummed to itself.

I looked around.

If I was not deceiving myself in the pervasive glow, the crimson walls curved away to each side as well as fore and aft. The chair and I waited in the center of a great cross, an intersection of crimson vaults.

A green oblong appeared to my right side.

The size of two men, it shone a refulgent greenness into the lambent crimson glow.

I bellowed.

"Is that you, Ahrinye?"

Ahrinye, a younger Star Lord, had made his opposition to the older Everoinye known. And younger and older. . . ? What meanings did those words have to beings whose life spans must run into the millions of years?

Dray Prescot

With a whining hiss another chair shot out of the green oblong.

It rushed past me.

It hurtled away along the crimson floor, heading the way I had come.

One glance was all I had, one look at the occupant of the other chair.

He, in his turn, had had one good look at me.

His numim roar lashed out as he whistled past.

"Zaydo! You no good rascal! Skulking again, are you—"

And then he was gone, Strom Irvil of Pine Mountain, gone whirling away. His glorious lion-man's face was in full flower, all his wounds healed. His fur, his hide, glowed more brightly than I had seen it before, when he'd been trapped in the bowels of the earth and sorely wounded. His bristling lion mane was a tawny umber. He roared with the righteous wrath of a great lord chastising a lazy body slave.

The body slave had been me, Zaydo, and Strom Irvil had been taken up before my eyes, taken up by the Everoinye.

Well, he'd come belting out of that green door.

I did not think he'd gone in there by choice.

Was it my turn next?

The chair moved.

Hissing, it curved past the green oblong. The greenness dimmed, dwindled, was gone.

I sucked in a breath.

Nothing like this had happened to me before.

The Star Lords had told me they were growing old. How old that might be was beyond my guessing. Were they becoming senile? Were they fumbling? They had made mistakes before. They had made a mistake with a time loop, and dropped me down into the wrong time, and, correcting that mistake, had given me all of Djanduin. Perhaps their powers were failing?

Anyway, they hadn't given me the Kingdom of Djanduin. That wonderful country had come my way first through boredom and then through duty. I was the King of Djanduin.

The chair passed on along the crimson floor, and the vaulting rolled past above, and the whitely glittering star constellations changed and glowed and shone with supernal fires.

Another chair passed, going by in a flicker of movement.

The occupant was a man, an apim like me, a member of *Homo sapiens*. I add the second *sapiens* in deference to our old friends the Neanderthals, who in these later times have become far more exciting than of yore. He sat hunched, looking ill. He was, as he would have to be to be a Kregoinye and perform the will of the Star Lords, a big strong fellow with a powerful face. His hair was long and blond and confined in braids beneath a steel helmet. Hs face bore the scars of battle. He wore a badge upon his chest, a thing of gold and silver threads in the form of a rampant graint. The ferocious crocodile-headed bear leered at me as the man whisked past.

He was gone, and I twisted my head around to stare after him.

He stared back at me, turning to look aft. He smiled.

I returned his smile.

This man, this blond warrior with the graint badge, was the third Kregoinye I had seen. The second was Strom Irvil. The first was Pompino, that foxy-faced Khibil of unusual talents, with whom I had shared many adventures. Would I encounter Pompino here? I looked forward to that meeting with genuine joy.

As for this third Kregoinye—his hard warrior face bore marks of illness, deeply indented lines, and a pallor that floated his tan like scabbed paint. What, I wondered, had happened to him? Then I banished all other thoughts, to concentrate on what was happening, as the chair bore me, with horrible suddenness, into total blackness.

Somewhere a loon laughed like a demented creature.

Or, more likely, someone screamed in torment.

Or, that horrendous noise could more likely be merely the hissing rush of the chair, screeching as it bore me on into the unknown.

Sparkling motes of light danced before me, thin and scattered at first, but thickening, dancing in clumps and gyrating nodules of fiery brilliance. We rushed on and through them, motes of diamond dust, brushing them aside in whirls of sparkling specklings. I drew a breath. The dots of light swung away from us. Rather, we swung away from them, surging out to hiss along an ebon floor, with all the sparkles massing and banking away to the left.

The chair stopped.

I turned my head away from the sparkles and looked to find what I expected to see.

Framed in their thick silver rims, three pictures adorned the far wall. Oval pictures, three of them in a line along the blackness, each showed a different face of the planet Kregen.

Silence dropped down. I could hear my harness creaking as I breathed, and that displeased me, a professional fighting man.

Each silver-framed picture showed an aerial view of Kregen. That on the extreme left showed the familiar outlines of Paz, the side of the world I knew.

There were the outlines of the continents of Havilfar, and Loh, of Segesthes and Turismond. The islands, too, showed clearly, Pandahem and Vallia—I stopped for a moment to dwell on Vallia. That small island at the eastern seaboard was Valka, with Veliadrin to the west. Valka! Well, my home was a long way off now, farther off even than from the flier taking Seg and me north across Hamal.

Funny. Here was I, looking down on a picture of Havilfar, and Seg and I were flying across that land.

He would be gripped in a stasis, unmoving, the butter knife in his hand, all unknowing of where I had gone.

But would he?

Perhaps he merely moved and had his being in normal time. Perhaps it was I who was speeded up in some weird way, sent spinning into the gulfs of superhumanity?

I shifted my gaze away from Paz and looked at the center picture.

This showed sea, with the hint of land at each horizon.

The extreme right hand picture showed a pattern of islands and continents I did not know—although a few of the ancient maps in the Akhram had hinted at such configurations.

I knew I was looking at a map of the other side of Kregen. I committed what I could to memory, as I had tried to do before, and a voice spoke in words and also in my head.

"Yes, Dray Prescot. Look well on the world of Kregen. It may be that you will have little time left to look on the world you call home."

Chapter Six

By this time I was past caring about how scared I was.

I said, "I suppose, Star Lords, you will as usual not bother to explain what you mean."

No answering laugh, a bubbling chuckle, hung on the scented air. I had thought that perhaps the Star Lords retained still some elements of a human sense of humor. But the feeling of coldness drove out laughter.

"We do not need to explain, Dray Prescot. It is not a case of bothering."

Well now. . . !

"Why do I have little time? Do you intend to send me . . ." My voice trailed. I did not want even to put into words the thought that I might be dispatched back to Earth.

The voice, in my ears and in my head, said, "We do not have a task for you to perform at the moment. We summoned you here to acquaint you with our desires for the future. Also, Dray Prescot, we wish you to know that we are well pleased that you have driven back the Shanks."

There was so much astonishing information in those few words, I sat back in the chair. The straps confining my arms had fallen away, and I had not noticed.

"You—" I said. Then: "You are thanking me?"

By Zair!

The Everoinye, omnipotent superhuman overlords, descending—condescending—to give a mere mortal human being a word of thanks!

Astonishing!

The Shanks, who by a variety of names were bad news, came raiding up over the curve of the world from their unknown homelands. They festered along the coasts of Paz. And they had tried to invade and settle, and we had beaten them and driven them back in the Battle of the Incendiary Vosks.

The voice whispered, "Yes, Dray Prescot. You beat the Shanks. But the Fishheads are not finished."

"That I know only too well."

"We thank you—and your astonishment offends us. Much has happened since you were first brought to Kregen by the Savanti. We are pleased that we discovered you and took you into our service. You have performed well. But if you think that your days of toil are numbered—"

"No, Everoinye," I said. And I let rip a gusty sigh. "I know I am a fool, an onker of onkers, but I'm not onker enough to believe that."

"We do not dispute your self-judgment that you are an onker."

I just let that ride by. At least, it did show that the Everoinye might still have a shaky grasp on a shoddy sense of humour.

"We said we were pleased you beat the Shanks. We did not thank you."

So that was one in the eye for me. I had presumed, and had presumed wrong.

"But we do thank you, as you pointed out by your astonishment. We are offended at ourselves, that we have fallen away from a humanity of which once we were proud."

"Once?"

The voice sharpened.

"We will not say—'still.' We are no longer human."

"You can say that again."

"We are not, Dray Prescot, less than human. We are superhuman."

Some note, some timbre, something, made me say, "You poor devils."

For a time, then, there remained silence between us.

At last the voice whispered: "Look at the—"

The word used meant nothing.

"Look," said the voice, and there was strained patience in its tones. "Look at the pictures on the wall. The right-hand picture."

I looked.

Whatever word the Everoinye had used to mean the pictures, I did not know it and couldn't reproduce it. Afterward, when I discovered alternative meanings for the word "screen," that still was not the word. That came much later.

So I looked and the continents and islands of the antipodes swam before my gaze.

"That configuration of lands is very like Paz. We call it Schan. It is a use name. The Fishheads who raid you in Paz sail from the coastal areas. There are many other peoples of the islands and continents. Unpleasant people. Now look at the center picture."

The sea sparkled blue, almost as though it moved and struck the suns light from wave tops.

I peered more closely and then, miraculously, the sea seemed to swarm away around each side of the picture. It was as though I were falling down into the oval frame.

I jerked back in the chair..

The sea came very near. It was clear and sparkling.

A fleet sailed that sea.

A fleet of squat, square, unlovely ships, with high poops and chunky bows, bristling with armaments. I knew the waterline would be sweetly curved, the underwater parts marvels of naval construction. The masts, tall, after the fashion of poleacres, bore the tall, narrow, slantingly curved sails of the Shanks. They did not so much catch the wind and belly out, as on ordinary vessels, as take the wind and plane it over their curves as the wind planes over a gull's wing.

"I see them," I said. "Fishheads, Leem-Lovers—"

"Yes. They sail to Paz. They follow the advance guard which you defeated on the sands of Eurys."

I shook my shoulders.

"I did not beat the Shanks alone. There were many with me, men and women, all brave and valiant, and all who shared in the victory—"

"Yes, yes. Paz turned out its finest."

"I would not forget that."

"The Shanks have been driven out of some of their homelands. They intend to take yours."

I put my fingers to my forehead, and rubbed.

By Krun! I was tired!

"I, for one, cannot condemn them for that."

"If you understood more, you would—"

"Mayhap. All the same, if they try to steal what belongs to Paz, they must be stopped. Or," I added, hoping for a miracle I knew would not be vouchsafed, "perhaps, they could be assimilated, somehow—we have lands they could settle."

"They intend to slay you all. They do not believe in half measures."

So the ugly business persisted, the desires of men that drove out all feeling, that blinded to all save personal gain.

"And," I said, and the weariness slurred my words, "in the half of the world you call Schan there are many more nasties behind the Shanks."

"Very many."

"Is there an end? Will it ever stop?"

"Yes."

"How?"

"When Kregen becomes as the Everoinye and the Savanti wish it to be. Those desires clearly conflict at the moment; when they are as one, the business will end."

"I thought the Savanti merely wished to make the world over—"

"The Savanti wish to make the world of Kregen a world for apims alone. We believed you understood that."

It had been there, a black thought in my mind, to be driven out and banished. Much had pointed to that reading of the way the Savanti operated. They sent their Savapims out into the world to preserve an apim way of life. They had recruited me from Earth, to be a Savapim, and I had failed them and been driven out—rather, I'd told them to keep their paradise and had escaped with Delia. Now I saw the truth. And I sorrowed, for I had loved the Savanti and their Swinging City of Aphrasöe.

I took a breath.

"This is bad news. Tell me, Everoinye, why do you open up these secrets to me now—?"

"We grow old, Dray Prescot."

The fear in me took a strange turn.

If the Star Lords could grow old, perhaps die, how would that affect the fate of Kregen?

"I have a thousand years of life because I bathed in the Pool of Baptism in Aphrasöe. You, Star Lords, must have many and many a thousand years of life—"

"If we have, you would do well to think that perhaps those thousands of years are not to be devoted to Kregen alone."

I felt shattered.

Then a thought came to me that might be connected.

I said, "You told me that the Savanti objected to what the Curshin did on Kregen—"

"Stop, Dray Prescot!"

The voice almost knocked me over with its power.

"You are a rogue, a miscreant, a man with a charisma that

can rouse whole nations to do your will and bidding with joy and gladness. But you may not speak of things that you cannot understand. We told you there are Others of whom we do not speak. The Curshin are not of these. But you do not speak of them."

Somehow I managed to keep my mouth shut.

The Star Lords went on speaking.

"There are forces driving on the Shanks, as we have told you, obvious forces. But there are Powers that drive on the forces that impel those that drive the Shanks. In these things, Dray Prescot, you may not meddle."

I burst out: "By Vox! I don't want to meddle in any of it! I just want to get the business finished!"

"And that is your task to perform. If you do it well, you may remain on Kregen."

"I'll do it," I raged. "By the disgusting diseased left nostril of Makki Grodno! I'll do it or get chopped in the doing—as you damned well know!"

"We know, Dray Prescot. We know. And—we know far more than you think we know of yourself; because you do not understand yourself at all."

By Zair! That was true—confound it. . . .

The arms of the chair began to writhe up. I guessed there was to be an end to this audience. I got a deep lungful of air and said in my old harsh way, "How long do we have before that enormous fleet of Shanks reaches us? And, where will they touch land?"

"As to the latter—that you must wait and see. As to the former—" Here the arms clamped me tightly. "You have a few seasons yet."

"Enough to—?"

"Enough to do what you want to do, what you know you must do. When the time is nearer, we will call on you again—if we do not call on you before that."

Was there that incongruous note of laughter that I have likened to the last bubble in a forgotten glass of champagne? The Star Lords, were they laughing at me?

The chair gripped me. The blackness swirled. All the stars of the galaxy went around in my head and Seg said, "Here, my old dom, catch hold of this bread, will you. The soup is almost done."

Chapter Seven

Into Pandahem

The pursuit continued all through the night.

The Moons of Kregen sailed majestically overhead, the stars massed into a pervasive glitter that reminded me uncomfortably of the spanning star-glitter in that crimson curved chamber, and Seg and I in comradely fashion took watch turn and turn about.

As we both half expected, the fleeing voller swung sharp left-handed after passing the northern coast of Hamal. She fleeted westward. Here we were practically on the Equator.

"Pandehem," said Seg. "Has to be."

"I agree. So there's no wager there."

Seg screwed up his face.

Our voller was making a speed equivalent to just under eighty miles an hour, a pretty fast clip for an airboat, but slow in comparison with some of the swift vollers in existence. We continued to head due west. Seg sniffed the breeze, and looked around from south to north.

Then he said, "No wager on Pandehem, that is true. But a wager on which part?" He laughed, his fey blue eyes very merry. "And any loon would suggest we are making for the southern half, I'll wager you we're headed for the northern."

That thought had been in my mind.

"Very well. I had a hankering for the north. They'll turn north, probably, and aim to bypass the Koroles. A due north-west course would suit them. So, I'll wager on the south."

"A gold double-talen?"

I nodded.

"Done."

Past Skull Bay and due west over the sea fleeted the voller. The day passed. We saw no signs of any other aerial traffic, although twice we passed above argenters, their fat sails bellying and their fat hulls punching into the sea.

60

We sat and talked and fiddled with our equipment and eyed the fleeing airboat.

"He makes no signs of changing course."

"He is well aware we are following."

"Of course. And," said Seg, "I'll wager he doesn't care!"

"You think he wants us to follow into a trap?"

"More than likely." Seg ran an oiled rag down a sword blade that had been polished to a blinding reflection. "He knows you're aboard."

"Maybe," I said, deliberately ignoring Seg's suggestion that if I were around then everyone would be setting traps for me. Mind you, by Vox, it was uncomfortably near the truth. . . . "I'd suggest he's a cautious navigator. He hugs the coast."

"Well, no one is stupid enough to fly northwest from Ruathytu, over the Western Hills and across whatever lies beyond. The wild men out there are plain murder."

"Yes. But it looks as though he's going to fly along the coast and then turn due north for Pandeham. Cautious to a degree."

"It could be," said Seg, looking up, "that he has one of the old Hamalian vollers that always broke down."

I nodded, realizing the justice of the suggestion.

Now that we had formed bonds of friendship with Hamal, we did not have to buy inferior airboats that continually broke down. But there were still a lot about, despite the losses of the Times of Trouble and the wars.

"If his flier does break down, we're nicely situated to go down and haul him out of the drink. And Pancresta."

But the voller we pursued did not falter in her onward rush through the air of Kregen.

Even at ten db* the journey took a goodly time and I said to Seg, fretfully, "You'd think the Hamalese would provide the fastest vollers for their guards. Nedfar evidently overlooked that."

"Had they done so, that flier up front would be going as fast as we are."

Good old Seg! Trust him to sort out the idiotic remark and upend it for all to see. In this case the all was me.

Then Seg stuck his face up, staring ahead.

"Hullo. He's changing course."

I joined Seg and we watched as the flier up ahead swung

---

*db: Dwaburs per bur. A dwabur is five miles approx and a bur is forty minutes approx. A.B.A.

gently around, not losing distance over a too-acute turn, and headed into the northwest.

"That course will—" Seg paused, and then went on—"take him between Wan Witherm and the Koroles. It looks like South Pandahem, after all."

We turned to follow.

"It's all jungles and stuff there, I believe."

"Well, he may fly on over the Central Mountains."

Settling down again to this stern chase, we brewed up, and ate some more of the rations. We estimated we could eat them all by the time we arrived at the south coast of the island of Pandahem. If the Spikatur people up front escaped from us over a simple matter like the lack of provender, we'd be looking silly.

"Tighten our belts, my old dom. They won't starve us into giving up the chase."

I laughed.

"They will more likely escape through a lack of potables in this voller—yes?"

And Seg laughed, too.

We found a brass-bound spyglass in one of the lockers and took turns staring after the voller ahead. I summed up her lines, seeing they were identical for all practical purposes to our own voller's. The differences were merely those of ornamentation. The reason why our speeds were so evenly matched was, therefore, simple. We all flew in the same breed of airboat.

"When I worked in the voller yards of Sumbakir," I said, "we built mostly personal fliers. But I recognize like and like. We'll not catch that fellow unless he does something extremely foolish."

"That may be. But he has to come down somewhere, some time. Then we'll drop down on top of him."

"Aye."

The air tanged with heat, now, the sea below a sweltering shimmer. The rush of the breeze blew as a solid wall of heat, hot and choking in our faces.

"Southeast Pandahem," I said. "I don't know that part of the world, Seg."

"I know nothing definite, either. There was a fellow I knew—a paktun with one ear missing and a ferocious squint, old Frandor the Schturmin—told me he'd once served a king or prince down in the southeast. Stinking jungles, he said. Potty as notors, the lot of 'em, so Frandor said."

"I can believe it."

Then Seg let rip his chuckling grunt of good humor.

"I agreed with him, too. That was before you made me a damned notor, a jen, and dumped me in it. All lords are stark staring bonkers. It is a law of nature."

"That," I said, and I spoke mildly, "I do not believe."

"No? Well, maybe. All I will say is that if the jungle is our destination, we'll sweat a trifle."

The dwaburs passed away, and as we had anticipated, the food ran out.

I eyed Seg.

He saw me looking at him.

I licked my lips.

"You look fat and healthy, Seg," I said. "I wonder how much seasoning you will need."

"You could put all the salt on my tail you liked, my old dom. I'd still be too damned stringy."

"As to that, that I do believe."

We almost lost our quarry in a build-up of clouds over the coast.

The voller ahead darted into a white canyon of billowing cloud. We followed, and we had the speed lever notched over past its rightful halting place. We held on; but it was a near thing.

Thunderstorms raged among the clouds.

Twice we were hurled end over end, and twice we righted ourselves, clinging on with gripping fingers, to hurl our voller on in pursuit.

The storms held us both up, pursuer and pursued alike, and presently the flier carrying Pancresta began a series of maneuvers which, apart from wasting time, gained them not a palm in distance upon us.

At last we broke free of the storms and the darkness and sailed on over jungle, steaming in the new radiance.

A wide river rolled along below, brown and smooth, carving its path through the forest.

"If you can believe what old Frandor the Schturmin told me, and if I'm right, that'll be the River of Bloody Jaws."

I nodded. There was no need to enlarge on who owned the jaws in the Kazzchun River.

"She flows down from the Central Mountains all the way to the Sea of Chem." Seg gestured over the coaming. "There is a fair amount of traffic."

On the broad brown surface boats moved, mostly propelled

by long sweeps all working in unison. There were a few more rakish craft tacking along. We saw a few small habitations in clearings along the banks. Whoever lived down there made what they could out of their surroundings.

We flew on, deeper into the island. Pandahem, like Vallia, in size is on the order of the size of Australia; there was a lot of it. Hereabouts, quite clearly, the river formed the main and best, possibly the only, means of communication.

Scraps of cloud drifted by. We saw flocks of water fowl, wide-winged and long-necked, rising in multitudes from the waters. Brown mudflats gleamed. On those banks the ominous forms of risslaca showed. No one was going swimming in the River of Bloody Jaws without regretting the notion.

"I don't expect to see any fliers here in Pandahem," said Seg. "But they must be known. The folk down there do not pay as much attention."

"Hamal and Hyrklana never would sell vollers to Loh or Pandahem, among others. Now we have these damned Shanks to fight I think the Pandaheem will get their vollers."

"They're surely needed in this part of the world."

We flew so grandly over the tops of the trees. What it would be like down there, trudging along, was something I did not wish to find out. Even the river for travel would be a headache.

Up ahead the forest lifted to a shallow range of hills. They were not mountains. But there were a lot of them, serried ranks of rounded slopes, one after another, and every one crammed with the ferocious vegetation of the jungle. The rain forest swarmed up over the rounded hills.

"The river trends away to the east," said Seg.

"I see. Is that a town near the beginning of the bend?"

Seg used the spyglass.

"Yes. Now, I wonder. . . ?"

But the voller flew on, over the town in its riverside clearing, on and rising to soar over the unending roundnesses of the jungle-clad slopes.

We no longer flew a trifle west of north following the course of the river as it rolled down southeast. Now we flew on over solid jungle.

Seg had the spyglass trained neatly on the voller.

I thought I glimpsed a flicker of movement among the trees ahead of the path of the voller.

There was just a sudden movement there, a hint of a cloud of black dots, and then the sky over the trees was clear.

"Seg! Train your glass down, ahead of the voller—there—there where that rounded hill slopes over that valley—"

He did as I said, instantly.

After a moment, he said, "I see only trees."

"I thought I glimpsed—something—there."

"Only trees, now."

He handed me the glass.

I looked. The tops of the closely packed trees jumped into focus. I was looking down onto the crowns of the denizens of a rain forest, and no prying with human eyes would descry what lay on the forest floor.

I handed the spyglass back.

"Nothing, save the trees. But—"

"Yes? What was it?"

I took a breath.

Seg believed I'd seen something.

"Like a flock of birds—"

"All right. Nothing unusual in that."

"Agreed. But at this distance—they must have been large—"

"Saddle birds?"

Seg's tone was sharp.

"Aye."

He looked seriously at me, his fey blue eyes regarding me calmly. "Pandahem does not have flyers."

"I know. So that means. . . ."

"I'll cast loose the guidance ropes. We'll be ready to go down at once."

"Good."

I stared eagerly at the airboat ahead.

But—but the wretched thing just went sailing on, flying high and fast, going pelting along. She just flew over whatever mysteries lay beneath. Perforce, we followed.

Taking up the spyglass I leaned over the coaming and studied the ground underneath. Rather—the tops of the trees. . . .

Anything could be concealed under that luxuriant foliage. We hurtled out over the rounded top of a hill, and on the far side a fair-sized lake opened out. The water was as brown as the waters of the River of Bloody Jaws. A few islands studded the surface. There were no boats. A few birds quarreled on a brown mud spit. The suns light glinted up off the water. Sounds rose, the birds, the roars of hunting beasts, the distant splash of water I took to be a waterfall.

Swiveling, as our voller flashed on, I looked aft.

The edge of the hill fell sheer into the lake. It was buttressed by tall columns of rock, grey and weatherbeaten and festooned with lianas. Birds cavorted here, too. A spume of white mist was just visible over a rising shaft of rock.

Even in the rush of the breeze, the strong and pungent smell of flowers stung my nostrils.

"Spiny Ribcrushers," said Seg. "Like syatras."

"They smell—juicy."

"That's right. They'll melt you down to your boot soles."

The lake whisked away below, the tall buttresses of rock vanished aft. Ahead the voller bore on steadily. The rain forest started on the very edge of the lake, and continued, unbroken. Probably there was a small tributary down there.

Seg put the control levers back on the guidance ropes and presently he called: "The hills are flattening out ahead. And we have the river back."

It was clear that the River of Bloody Jaws, coursing down to the southeast, made a vast loop to go around this outcropping of hills.

I stared ahead, far into the distance.

There was no sign of the Central Mountains.

Still the voller sailed on.

At the apex of the curve of the river where it turned to skirt the jumbled upheaval of forest-clad hills stood a town. As we flashed past above we could see the town was stockaded, small but neat, with jetties extending into the river. There was no sign of a single vessel. Smoke rose and the smells of cooking lifted. Seg made a face and rubbed his stomach.

"Old Frandor told me they were a devilishly mixed bunch here, with screaming cannibals in one valley and a high level of civilization in the next. Something to do with the difficulties of communication after the old empire went."

"We saw something of that in the Hostile Territories—Seg? You remember?"

And then I wished I hadn't mentioned the Hostile Territories of Turismond and thus brought up memories of our adventures there. Delia and me—and Seg and Thelda. I said at once, "Look! The fellow's turning!"

Whatever made the voller carrying Pancresta choose that moment to turn, I blessed. Whatever it was saved me from a nasty moment.

Seg said, "He's turning gently—now what is he up to?"

We began to edge out to starboard to cross the angle of the other flier's turn and so meet him. But he was a clever flier and kept away, using all his speed, turned so that soon we were heading directly back the way we had come.

And, still, we followed.

But we had narrowed the gap considerably. If only we'd had a couple of db's more speed—but that was foolish. If we'd had those, we'd have caught Pancresta hours ago.

The reciprocal course was taking us away to one side of the town over which we had passed. Speeds in the air are phenomenal if compared with speeds on land.

Seg abruptly stiffened. The spyglass twitched and was held, rigid. He stared ahead.

Then he said, "You were right about the saddle flyers."

Of course! Pancresta's flier had shot on ahead, over that lake and the rearing columns of rock where I'd imagined I'd seen flyers. The voller had drawn us on, and then gently turned, taking all the time needed, and reversed course. The saddle flyers had risen in a cloud to follow.

And now we were heading smack back into them.

Very carefully, I said, "I think Pancresta will escape. I count thirty birds. By the time we've finished with them, she'll be gone."

"I think you are right." Seg picked up his two longbows, letting the spyglass fall. He looked at each one. "We'll feather them, all of them, I have no doubt. But that scheming woman will be vanished."

"We know where to, though. We'll find her."

"Aye, my old dom. We'll catch up with her, in due time. But, now—" And here Seg selected a bow and drew it gently, and so took an arrow and set nock to string—"now we have a fight on our hands."

Chapter Eight

Seg Quenches a Fire

Shooting through the windrush of a voller's flight is a truly difficult business. Seg had little difficulty aiming with the uncanny marksmanship of a Master Bowman of Loh. Seg had finished off my training as a bowman, after my ferocious Clansmen of Segesthes had taken me in hand, and I tried to match Seg, shaft for shaft.

"One gold piece, Dray, or—perchance—three?"

The wind caught at his dark hair, tumbled the locks over his forehead. His fey blue eyes challenged me right heartily. The wind blew, the hostile saddle birds dropped upon us—and, as ever, Seg was out for a wager or two, a side bet on the outcome in addition to our own lives.

"Three, I think," I said with a judiciousness that brought a delighted curl to Seg's lips.

Up aloft the birds winged in.

They sparkled with light. Radiance reflected from burnished accoutrements. The leading saddle flyer bore brilliant golden ornamentation over his breast feathers. That gold would be wafer-thin, beaten out into hollow shapes, strapped on with narrow leather bands. His wings held stiff in the attacking dive.

Seg sniffed, looking up. "Brunnelleys," he said. He held the new bow down, relaxed, the shaft crossing the stave and beginning that smooth draw of the master bowman.

The wind buffeted into our faces. The birds up there, gaudy of color in mauves and blues and browns, with yellow beaks and scarlet clawed feet—all four legs bore claws—swooped with that eager pounce of the brunnelley. Powerful saddle birds, brunnelleys, and like just about any other kind of saddle flyer unknown in the island of Pandahem.

"Aye. And the riders are not flutsmen, either."

"No. I fancy Spikatur has a hand in this." And then Seg lifted the bow, drew and loosed.

The shaft missed.

I looked not so much amused as dumbfounded.

In his turn, Seg looked at the bow. His brows drew down. He pursed up his lips. I shot and put a shaft through the wing of a brunnelley which wasn't going to do the bird a great deal of harm.

Seg threw the bow down into the bottom of the voller.

He picked up the other bowstave, and shook it.

"Thus do the prideful take a tumble, and the mighty are cast down. The stave does not cast true."

I knew he had no stupid boastfulness in equating himself with pride and mightiness; just that the aphorism fit and appealed to our sense of humor. With his second cast he sent the shaft clean through the breast of the rider.

The fellow screeched and fell off, to dangle all upside down in the straps of his clerketer under his bird's tail feathers.

"H'm," quoth Seg. "That is marginally better," and so shot again, thwack thump and sent a shaft clean through the eye of the next.

I tried to match my companion; but when Seg got himself into a paddy and shot with real intent, there was no man alive on two worlds, I devoutly believe, who came within a million dwaburs of him.

We began to take the diving formation apart, and such was the ferocity of our shooting the plunging birds parted and screamed down with whistling feathers on either side of our voller.

That was merely round one.

In the brief respite before the next attack we glimpsed Pancresta's flier diving steeply ahead, going down with tremendous speed to soar out over the river.

"They're gone," said Seg, arranging his next series of shafts in the quick-release sockets along the gunwale.

"Aye. For now."

"Here they come again."

Once more we shot sufficiently well to drive off the attack. Four shafts plunked into the woodwork of the voller, and a handful more cut through the canvas.

We were aware of height and wind and of rushing progress through the air. The Suns cast light and shadow, and the birds wheeled about us now, their riders shooting down. One or two cast javelins, but I made no attempt to snatch a javelin from the air and hurl it back. At this moment the bow was the superior weapon.

Our voller ploughed on, slowing down, surrounded by the furious cloud of birds.

"They thin out." Seg shot and took up shaft and drew and shot again.

"True."

I put my head over the coaming and looked down.

"The rasts."

Half a dozen riders closed in on their birds, the wings beating perilously close together, aiming to strike up at our exposed underside.

Three quick shafts took three of them out; but the balance bored on. Golden ornaments glittered. The men riding the birds hunched in tightly buckled cloaks, not streaming flamboyantly, and their small round helmets gleamed with purpose. This group carried crossbows. A bolt punched up through the canvas past my nose, and I jumped back.

"I count that as three gold pieces to me," said Seg, and he laughed.

"Indubitably." I looked over again, in time to put a shaft into the nearest fellow. He looked up with the utmost surprise on his face, one-eyed, for the shaft through the other one impeded his vision somewhat.

He fell off his bird, and the brunnelley curved away, carrying the dangling rider like a pendulum clock.

Seg sniffed.

At once disabused of the notion that he was passing a comment on my shooting, I sniffed also.

We looked quickly about.

Shafts hissed in, to feather into the voller and start to turn her into a flying pincushion.

Smoke blew flatly back.

"They've set us afire, my old dom. But where is the flame?"

Smoke suddenly choked back in a great evil-smelling cloud.

"Wherever it is, the wind drives it flat, and the smoke obscures the source."

Then I cursed myself for a ninny, a nincompoop, for the kind of man no captain of a seventy-four would ever employ as his first lieutenant. When I served in the Royal Navy of Nelson's time we habitually doused fires before going into action, and sanded the decks, and took the utmost precautions against being set alight.

And, now, I'd just forgotten to douse the fire in the combustible box, and it had been struck by a shaft, and overturned, and set our voller aflame.

Even as this stupid, time-wasting self-recrimination echoed in my silly old vosk-skull of a head, the fire burst up and enveloped the voller. Flames blew flatly aft. Seg yelled.

He leaped for the controls and threw off the guidance ropes. He shoved the levers down and the flier's nose dropped and we fell out of the sky like a brick.

A flashing glimpse of a bird, upside down and with a broken wing where we'd struck him—a man slashing with his long flexible aerial spear—another fellow loosing and his bolt splintering into the coaming under my nose—and then we were hurtling down and down toward the ground.

We had no flying safey belts. We'd have to ride the voller down.

"Hold on!" bellowed Seg.

A gusting mass of smoke and flame billowed up, a choking confused mass, orange and scarlet and black, coiling and hot—damned hot!

The spectacle we must have made from higher up as the men astride their brunnelleys looked down surely convinced them we were doomed.

I wasn't too sure myself. . . .

"Seg!" I bellowed.

My comrade towered amid the filthy smoke, enveloped in flame, a titanic figure of myth, of the time when men walked among volcanoes and leaped the fire-filled chasms in the earth.

He yelled back, and the words blustered past, lost amid wind and smoke and flame roar.

The trees reared up.

What Seg did with the controls was what any competent aerial pilot would do. He set them for a slanting impact, slowing the speed as much as he could, and then fastened the guidance ropes back on. But, being Seg Segutorio and a wild and fey fellow, he set the voller to a steeper angle than any more circumspect flier would risk.

We went skipping through the tops of the trees.

Tree branches thwacked at us, ripping canvas and gonging against wood.

Leaves fluttered up into our faces, birds squawked and flew

for safety, a horde of little red spiders wafted off on balloons of silk. A leafy bough slashed at my head and I ducked and my helmet reverberated as though the Bells of Beng Kishi were all cracked and dissonant.

We toppled out of the last hoary heads of the trees and pitched for the brown river below.

The voller was now a roaring combustible mass and Seg and I crouched in the stern, shielding our faces, waiting for the moment of impact.

Seg gasped out: "I thought—the river—douse the flames—"

Before I could cough out an answer we hit.

We felt as though we'd leaped off a roof onto a brick factory. The thump rattled through the flier, through our backbones and shook the teeth in our jaws.

Water fountained up around us, like a flower's petals, brown and silver, and we were hurled headlong into the water. Even then the hem of Seg's tunic caught alight and hissed madly as he went under.

We splashed to the surface, blowing suds, winded, blinded, singed, our heads ringing and ringing. I felt as though a torturer from the Empress Thyllis's dungeons under the Hammabi el Lamma had been at work on me for a sennight.

Seg whisked the water from his eyes and glared about.

"Back to the bank, sharpish!" I yelled.

We started splashing back.

The flier, burning, drifted away, and the flames flared for a long time before they were doused, as we could see by the reflections.

Over arm we crawled for the bank. Only two fang-jawed creatures had a go at us, and we managed to get a sword down in time to poke them off. They were not harmed. Their scales glistened in the light of the Suns and the licking fire reflections from the burning voller. The smell of the river began to get up our nostrils to replace the stink of smoke. That smell was all dark brown.

Rotting vegetation, slimed mud, bursting gas bubbles all joined in an infernal soup of aromas.

Seg reached the bank first. He grasped at a root sticking into the water and the damned thing came alive and tried to bite him.

He yelped and drew back and swiped at the thing.

It screeched and scuttled off on a hundred or so bandy

legs. It turned its flat head as it went, and its eyes promised that it would be back.

We crawled out and flopped face down on mud.

We breathed in and out, and we were alive, and that was miracle enough.

Up aloft against the bright haze there was no sign of the flyers astride their golden-adorned brunnelleys.

The first thing Seg said was, "I regret losing that stave that cast crooked. I would dearly have loved to find out why."

I said, "All I know is that shot gives me three gold pieces."

"We will work the reckoning as soon as we can. I do not recommend swimming in harness—although you, Dray Prescot, are half fish in the water."

"And you—half waterlogged tree trunk?"

He laughed and tossed his head and the water spun from his helmet. We believed in wearing armor, and we believed in wearing as much and as little as would protect us and let us move. I stood up and my foot went into the mud knee deep. A stink gushed.

Hauling my leg out made a loud sucking noise.

"Inland a bit, and then head for the town?"

"Aye."

We lay sprawled for a few moments longer, getting our breath. Our equipment carried on our persons was still with us. That in the voller was gone past redemption.

Eventually we crawled off the mud and onto the first of the less squelchy ground. Trees struggled for existence and the light dimmed to a watery greenness. Rain forests can be gloomy places. The noises of hunting animals—those who hunted by day—echoed among the trunks and from the masses of leaves overhead. There was no real undergrowth. Walking was a matter of selecting a good line, of keeping the eyes wide open and of constantly rotating the head. Seg fussed with his bow, spanning a new string from the watertight pouch. I carried a drexer in my hand. We marched.

We spoke little. Sounds carried even among the maze of trunks. And we walked softly.

If I say without either pride or humility that we two pacing through the forest were probably more dangerous than any animal we were likely to meet, I believe you will understand, and realize that that is the way of it on Kregen—if you wish to survive.

Chapter Nine

Jungle Cabaret

Attacks from nasties of the forest came at infrequent intervals. Hereabouts the going was only really difficult where a tree had fallen, taking others with it, and so opened a gap in the canopy of leaves above. Here sunshine could pour down—and with twin suns the extent was measurably greater—and produce a twisted tangle of undergrowth.

Negotiating these places was really cutting a way through jungle.

Here it was, slashing with swords to carve a path, ducking vines and treacherously looping strands of animate vegetable killers, that the risslacas, the dinosaurs, attacked. Their smaller brethren also came panting after our blood.

We did not make a fuss about it.

As Seg, drawing out a fresh arrow and fitting nock to string, said, "They're only doing what Nature intended and trying to fill their bellies."

"Aye. It is their misfortune they choose us for dinner."

"I feel sorry for them. But. . . ."

And he loosed and blotted out the yellow glaring eye of a risslaca whose fanged jaws would, had they closed over either of us or both of us together, have chopped us in half for a neat midday snack.

I loosed to take out another, smaller, dinosaur.

They humped along between the tree trunks, adapted to this environment either by nature or by genetic engineering, and we jumped down into a ravine, choked with vines. The emerald and ruby light lay across the clearing, and the dazzle above precluded looking at the sky.

In this slot of jungle-choked forest we encountered a couple of hairy crachens, and managed to drive them off, their mandibles waving, without killing them. Their faceted eyes

74

regarded us. I took from them the same impression I'd taken from the multi-legged pseudo tree-branch on the bank.

Those eyes said—We'll be back.

Tiny pinhead stingers wrung blood from us, and we had to beat them off, flickering, clinging, clouding wings gauzy in the dim light. Their life span might only be a day or so; they lived it up while they could, and drank their blood off with the best.

Although had it happened it would not on Kregen have been at all unusual, I have to report that we did not find a single princess to rescue from a dinosaur. Or find a single princess, come to that. We plunged on, through the rough areas and going as fast as we could with caution between the aisled trunks of the trees. Old, those trees, old and anciently hoary, festooned with parasitic growths, lush with tree-borne life, and of a normal human scale in height. But they were growing on the island of Pandahem, alongside the River of Bloody Jaws—on Kregen—and, although like jungly trees of Earth, they were different, very different.

When we reached a recognizable trail we halted.

From the cover of a tree trunk we looked out.

His voice pitched so that it would reach me and not listening hostile ears, Seg gave his opinion.

"Well—I'm not walking along *that!*"

"No."

He cocked his head at me.

"Ten gold pieces I spot a trap first."

"Done."

In his home in Erthyrdrin, at the northern tip of the continent of Loh, Seg had lived a pretty wild life before going as a mercenary to earn a living. Out there feuds rankled and a fellow had to keep his wits about him. Seg would probably spot a trap first—unless my own training with my clansmen, and with my Djangs and sundry other rascals and ferocious warriors of Kregen could aid me.

We paced the trail, well away among the trees, following its line. It was headed for the town.

Where it went the other way we did not know, for we'd come across it almost at right angles. It struck inland away from the river.

In any event we both said, "There!" and pointed together.

Instantly, we were both flat on our faces, alongside each other and head to tail, glaring out.

But nothing stirred.

After a time—a goodly time, for to rush in these matters is to court disaster—we stood up and inspected the trap.

"A tie, I think."

"Aye."

"Although I fancy your finger pointed after mine—"

"Never in a month of She of the Veils!"

Wrangling happily, we checked out the trap.

It was a simpleminded enough affair, a pit covered with leafy branches and positioned where enough sunlight dropped through an ancient and almost covered gap to give life to a little lower vegetation around. Simple it might be. It would be effective if anyone—be it animal or idiot human with no right to be wandering around in the jungle—should try to walk across it.

We went on.

A species of medium-sized vosk—larger than a bosk—lived here in the forest, rooting around, and no doubt the trap was laid for them.

They were wild, not domesticated, and they flourished a set of tusks that would part stomach from backbone in a trice.

We debated.

"Not worth it," I said.

"We-ell," said Seg. "I'm sharp set."

"The town cannot be far. They'll have vosk all ready cooked, crisp and golden and with momolams, too. . . ."

"I'll grant we wouldn't have to cook the meal. If the town doesn't show up in a bur or so, I shan't wait."

"Momolams?"

These are the splendid small round golden vegetables, rather like brand-new potatoes with mint and steaming with flavor, that can melt the saliva from granite.

"I tell you, Dray Prescot, if we reach this town and order up a meal of vosk and there are no momolams, I shall seriously consider marmelizing you."

"I am surprised to hear you voice so uncouth a word."

"Yes, it is fit only for savages. But, in these circumstances—"

And then we both held, stark still, poised, as voices floated in from the trees. Laughing voices, shrilling, and with the voices the sounds of bottles and glasses—surely, bottles and glasses?

Cautiously, we crept forward.

The funny thing is, and I was well aware that we might at any moment be fighting for our lives, I was thinking that the

golden-yellow tubers, these famous momolams, are more often eaten with roast ponsho than with vosk. We reached a
crusty-barked tree and hunkered down, and slowly, cautiously, looked around, one each side.

The trail lay nearer to Seg than to me. I saw a small clearing, uncluttered with undergrowth except for a strange plant
rather like a large gourd, from the top of which extended a
thick stalk crowned with an orange flower.

From the gourd section came the sound of voices and the
rattle of bottle lip against glass.

Perhaps Seg made more noise than I did. Perhaps because
he was just the nearer of the two of us. . . . As lean and
tough as I was, he would have been no juicier. . . .

I stared out on the strange plant.

Certainly the gourd was of a size to hold two or three
people. But I did not think two or three people were inside
having a party. The stem bearing its orange flower lifted
some fifteen feet from the top of the gourd, swaying gently
five meters or so up, and as I took all this in, and realized
what this was all about, so I was yelling my head off and
jumping forward, sword raised.

"Seg!"

The stem lashed.

The orange flower opened, revealing massed spines.

It struck. It struck full at Seg's head.

I roared in, just bashing in a full-shouldered charge at the
stem, and with the sword slashing and hacking, cutting
through the fibrous vegetable growth. Thick green liquid
gushed. The flower writhed. It twisted in on itself, blindly
seeking its tormentor. I took a tremendous swing and the
steel bit and then the flower hit me a thwack across the
shoulder and head over heels I went into the muck.

It seemed to me only a moment or two later that a
woman's voice said, "Well, pantor Seg, your friend is alive, it
seems."

And Seg's voice, as though from a distance: "For which I
give thanks to Erthyr the Bow, and to all the Lords of
Creation." And, then, because he was Seg Segutorio, and the
truest blade comrade a man could ever hope for, he added,
"And, anyway, he has the skull of a vosk and the hide of a
boloth, the speed of a leem and the strength of a zhantil."

The woman laughed.

"I see you two get on together."

"I owe him ten gold pieces for this one—"

I tried to open my eyes, and the woman's voice sharpened.

"You would pay him ten gold croxes for saving your life? Is that what you value yourself at?"

"No, mistress Tlima, it is a bet I lost."

"I see—"

But, it was clear, she did not see at all.

The glue holding my lids down parted with some pain and light flooded in. I blinked, and Seg said, "About time."

Just to keep him going, I said, "Ten gold crox pieces, and not clipped, either."

He laughed.

His laugh rang out, joyous, full.

I sat up.

When my shoulder returned and attached itself to my body, I went to give it a rub, and the woman put a hand out and stopped me.

"Leave it, pantor. It is bandaged."

She was apim, full of face and figure, wearing a dark blue gown with white lace, and her features were those of a woman who has fought through life, and sees some comfort before they ship her off to the Ice Floes of Sicce.

We were in a tavern, with a thatched roof and wooden beams, with wooden walls and wooden floor, and the furniture was plain and simple and clean. I ached all over.

"The poison. A single spine struck past the edge of your armor." Seg shook his head. "Well, you cannot armor every inch of your body and still prance about."

"No."

The orange flower in striking back at me, so Seg related, hit my shoulder where the armor stopped the poisoned spines dead. But a petal flapped up and that solitary damned spine ripped in past the rim of my corselet, past the mesh, and so nicked me in the neck.

"You'd have had your head fall off if I hadn't kissed your neck as though you were a luscious sylvie."

"I trust you enjoyed the experience."

"I am not a fellow for sylvies, as you know."

"You suggested it."

"I was merely trying to be vivid in describing what could have been more awkward if that damned flower thing had upended you."

"Oh? I see."

The woman, this mistress Tlima, looked on in a bewildered fashion.

She addressed us as "pantor" which is the Pandahem way of saying lord. It equates with the notor of Hamal and the jen of Vallia. She called Seg Seg. She did not name me.

By this time Seg knew that I had a whole arsenal of names on which I could call. And for the Emperor of Vallia to be swanning about in a jungle on Pandahem could be awkward for said emperor if avaricious minds got to work.

The gourd emitting its party noises and the orange poison-spined flower formed a symbiosis of plants dedicated to catching and eating people. They grew in handy spots. The Kregish name can most easily be given as the Cabaret Plant.

Cabaret, I think, has the air to suit what they were up to.

Mistress Tlima bent and solicitously pulled and punched at my pillow in the way women have. A tinge of color glowed across her cheekbones.

"The Cabaret Plants are evil to us, for they delude poor drunken folk. Otherwise they live on small animals and their roots."

"Evil?" said Seg, raising one ferocious eyebrow.

"Yes!"

"As to that," I said, and rolled aside to avoid a sharpish straight left to the pillow and then rolled back to dodge the following right hook. "As to that, if a poor deluded folkim is drunk, perhaps he shouldn't be?"

"I shall fetch a meal," said mistress Tlima. The small room in which I lay was furnished as I have said, and was clearly one of her superior guest rooms. Seg had paid her in good gold deldys, which are Havilfarese coins. The local gold coin, the crox, was named after the local king. He, I was to learn, was busy causing the dickens of a stir and an uproar that was to embroil Seg and me willy-nilly. So, I lay back on the severely mauled pillow and smiled up at my blade comrade.

"So you brought me in on your back, hey?"

He looked shifty for a moment, did Seg, and then he hauled out his purse and dished out the ten gold pieces.

"I'll hand it to you, Dray. You spotted that trap first."

I took the gold and let a big smirk contort my features. That rubbed the salt in. Seg suddenly burst out laughing. He gazed down on me as the door opened and mistress Tlima came in with the tray that, quite clearly, had been already prepared. Still laughing, Seg burst out: "You can smirk all you like, Dray! I'm only thankful to have lost the ten deldys! By the Veiled Froyvil! I thought I was consigned to the Ice Floes of Sicce then."

Mistress Tlima placed the linen-covered tray on the side table. She stared reproachfully at Seg.

"Pantor Seg! How could you?"

"Well," said Seg, and that shifty look returned, "you can't afford to give this comrade of mine a knuckle."

"Pantor Dray? He saved you, and you tell him you brought him in all the way through the forest on your back!"

"Oh?" I said. I was enjoying this. "Oh ho?"

"You can oh ho, and oh ho ho, my old dom—I'll tell you—Mistress Tlima's husband came across us and we brought you in flopped out over the back of his cart."

So, I laughed.

By Zair! But it was good to be alive!

The food was good. It was roast rashers of vosk, juicy and crisp, all at the same time. And—momolams. Also there was a pottery dish of palines, and this sovereign berry, cure for melancholy as for dyspepsia, grew just as luxuriously in the rain forests of Pandahem as in the sweet lands of my own Valka.

When she had gone, and the door was closed, mistress Tlima remained Seg's chief concern.

"I had not realized—"

"It is of no consequence."

"But—"

"Perhaps, Seg, I have had my fill of running around under a score of different names. I am Jak—true. But also I am called Dray. And so I shall be."

He sniffed, resigned.

"By Vox! I am glad I don't have to keep track of all your names."

But we both knew the old truth that if you wanted to stay alive on Kregen you had to remember names. If you didn't, you were like to get killed pretty sharpish.

By the next day I was recovered enough to venture on a gentle stroll around this jungle town of Selsmot. I commented that calling the place a smot—meaning town—was rather grand. The stockade kept out the forest, and there was really, all things considered, a fine area maintained free and growing vegetables. The houses of wood and thatch and leaf were open and airy and a surprising number of them crowded within the stockade. But, all the same, the place was run-down and apathetic.

Seg said, "That's because old King Crox has gone missing and no one has the heart—"

"Gone missing?"

We walked along the dusty street—when it rained the dust became a quagmire—and Seg told me what he had discovered.

A band of most unhealthy bandits—drikingers—hung out in the bend of the river among those rolling tree-clad hills over which we had flown in pursuit of Pancresta. King Crox had taken in a strong expedition to deal with them once and for all. Nothing had been heard from him since, and that was two seasons ago. So—he had gone missing.

"Chopped," I said. "Poor fellow."

Then, sharply, I swung about to face Seg, saying, "And a band of drikingers in the jungle—that adds up to—"

"Perhaps. Pancresta and Spikatur—"

"It has to!"

"Except that although the king has gone missing, the drikingers have stopped plundering the trails and the river. He must have been successful."

"Very well." I could see from Seg's manner there was more. "Go on, you great infuriating—bowman—"

"The queen was determined to find the king. There was no love in it, so I am told, rather pride. She was married off for political reasons and the king rode off that night and—"

I smiled. "Not all women are beautiful nor all men handsome."

"This Queen Mab went after the king with her own expedition and—"

I cocked my head up. "She's gone missing too?"

"Aye."

"And some fat regent will be running the country to the benefit of his pocket."

"Kov Llipton—"

"And that gives me even greater assurance that it has to be Spikatur Hunting Sword in the jungle. This Kov Llipton is probably in league with them and the drikingers."

"You, Dray Prescot, have a tortuous and mistrusting mind."

"Useful, at times."

"Oh, aye, useful."

Still there was a hint of mischief about Seg, a bubbling enjoyment of tantalizing me. I did not scowl—Seg was fully entitled to his bit of harmless fun. And, anyway, I did not feel the same urgency. I was feeling slothful. That, mistress Tlima had warned Seg, was the inevitable result of being poisoned by the Cabaret Plant, the final outcome of which was death. Seg had sucked out the poison, there had not been a full flower-freight of spines to strike me, and I was alive. But I was tired.

"Go on then, you will tell me as and when—"

He nodded toward a tumbledown building standing a little back from the line of the other buildings. The place leaned comfortably against an enormous tree, a single intruder from the jungle. Small agile forms sported among the branches. A warm friendly smell wafted from the building, and a hanging pottery jug outside proclaimed the nature of its business.

A few drops of warm rain fell.

In mere moments the deluge would thunder down, and the dusty street would squelch not just underfoot but halfway up our legs. People walked briskly for shelter.

"The Dragon's Roost," said Seg.

"Very good. I need a wet inside me more than outside."

Starting off for the tavern with its low leafy roof and leaning walls of solid trunks, I made Seg step out smartly to follow. There was more to this. He caught me up and we ducked our heads to pass under the curved beam over the open front door. The sound of people talking and the gusty smell of a variety of drinks met us, mingled with the odors of rich cooking and the tang of woodsmoke.

"There is a party of adventurers here, in The Dragon's Roost. They may be braggarts, they may be fools, they may be heroes, but they are determined to chance their fortune among the hills."

The low door gave onto a long enclosed stoop, bowered in greenery, a place sheltered from the heat of the Suns and the rain which, hot and thick, hissed down outside.

We looked at each other.

Seg beamed and I nodded, pleased.

"Right, Seg. They are out to make their fortunes in the hills. They know something, then, that we do not. And we will go along with them. It seems to me that they and us—we all have the same objective, I'll wager."

"That, my old dom, is one wager I'll not take on!"

Chapter Ten

At The Dragon's Roost

If we imagined we had only to march up the shallow steps to the stoop and enter The Dragon's Roost and join up with the expedition, we were quickly disappointed.

The obstacle stood, four square at the top of the steps, and glowered upon us.

He appeared to be apim, at least, through the hair that sprouted from every possible point, although his apimishness was not certain. His eyes, most merry and bright, belied the scowl twisting his hair-girt mouth. He showed uneven teeth, yellowed and missing biting chompers here and there, giving him a mouth like the side of one of Nelson's frigates.

"Clear off! Schtump! We've had enough rascals like you to stuff a vosk pie for the feast of Beng Hravimond!"

Our clothes had been in a state of wreckage after our burning and river adventures, and the trek through the jungle, so we had borrowed ordinary clothes from mistress Tlima. These were simple brownish tunics, reaching to above the knee, and open at the throat. Seg carried his bow and a quiver, and I my drexer. We looked, I suppose, ruffians.

"We are not masichieri," declared Seg, somewhat heatedly.

The mass of hair within the leather and metal harness did not give him time to continue.

"Masichieri, thieving rascals, rogues—schtump!"

Seg sighed.

"I do not want to teach this hairy flea-bitten mass a lesson. But, by the Veiled Froyvil! He leaves me precious little alternative."

"Tsleetha-tsleethi," quoth I, which is to say, softly-softly. "If he serves his belly, he merely does his duty."

The bright eyes regarded us more closely.

"Comedians, are you?"

"Your name, dom?" I said.

"I should be angry—but you amuse me. I am Hop the—"

"Hairy?" cut in Seg.

"Fambly! One more crude remark and I shall be forced to come to handstrokes with you—I am Hop the Intemperate."

"Ah!" I said wisely.

"What does that mean?"

"It means," said Seg, "that you are well named."

A girl's laugh intruded. We all turned to look along the stoop, and Hop the Intemperate immediately went into the full incline, his nose rubbing the floorboards, his massive bottom upended.

This kind of bowing and scraping has never pleased Seg or me, so we merely gave the girl a slight polite nod, more, I fancy, in acknowledgment of her beauty than anything else at that time.

She was pretty, rather than beautiful, with a pert nose and red lips. Her hair, of a light corn color, fell in a loose mass to one side, gathered in by a silver band. She wore a green tunic, simple in cut, girt by a silver belt. She carried only a dagger as a personal weapon; but I had no doubt that her other weapons had done the business for many a fine upstanding young fellow. She looked—winsome, I suppose is a good way to describe her. She was not, I judged, the queen of these parts.

"Stand up, Hop, for the sweet sake of Pandrite and his holy mother!"

Hop gathered himself, rather like a sheepdog shaking after a dip in the millpond. He glowed.

"Lady Ilsa!"

She looked at us.

The little dip between her eyebrows darkened.

That—and I sighed to myself—that was a familiar sign.

Her voice, cool, distant, commanding, reached us with the touch of a stroking feather over an open wound.

"And you are?"

Seg spoke up.

"Llahal, young lady—"

"Have you noticed," I remarked in a casual conversational way, "how they don't bother with a polite Llahal as a greeting in this benighted place?"

The girl gasped. She drew herself up, not flinching as much as expressing distaste and hauteur. Hauteur, a comical concept to an honest sailorman, ill-suited her.

Hop the Intemperate blew out, hard, making his whiskers shiver in the breeze.

"Now, then, you rogue—"

"All right, Hop. You have a job to do. This girl—"

She shouted, cutting off my undoubtedly hot-headed and foolish comments. She screamed. She shrieked for the guards and for Hop to take off our heads— Well, it was a silly vapid scene. Poor old Hop the Intemperate went to sleep, very gently, on the warped boards of the stoop. The first guard, a Gon whose shaven head glistened with butter-shine, jumped onto the stoop waving a spear and Seg's bow lined up—exactly.

The second guard crashed into the first, who was trying to run backwards, and the pair fell over.

Lady Ilsa stood, her fists jammed into her mouth, her eyes goggling.

I did feel sorry for her. Sincerely.

Seg said, "We are here to join the expedition. If these guards are going along, maybe we'd better think again."

"Lady Ilsa," I said, and I own I spoke rather sharpish. She jumped as though goosed. "We are friends; at least, we want to join the expedition. You'd better tell your guards to stand down, and quickly, before they are hurt."

She took her fists away from her mouth. She was shaking.

"You—!"

"We are honest fellows needing a job—"

A young gallant, dressed all in a glittering blue, with much gold embroidery, stepped out. His fists were thrust down on his hips. I noticed he was wearing a rapier and left-hand dagger, still unusual at that time on Pandahem. His face was of that pale, aristocratic, hollow, blot-faced self-possession which conceals homicidal characteristics from those who do not wish to look closely upon wealth and position.

"Ilsa? You are safe?"

He kicked the two guards who were groveling away around each other, trying to stand up, their harness in some unfathomable way inextricably intertwined. They made mewling noises. The young dandy kicked them again. He enjoyed that.

Seg started to say, "Llahal, notor. We wish to join—"

The young lord said, "Do not speak to me until I speak to you, offal."

He turned back to the girl, cutting Seg and me out of the world's existence. It was handsomely done, if overdone.

Seg glanced at me, and I smiled, and then we both laughed.

A new voice, a mellow, full voice, not quite a fruity voice, said, "At last. Some excitement to liven things up."

We looked along the stoop.

The owner of the opulent voice half-concealed his face with a large—a very large—yellow kerchief. He was dressed in a simple tunic of dark blue, so dark as to be called black save for the artfully inserted panels of royal blue. He carried no weapons. He sneezed. At once the woman at his side jumped forward with a sprig of the lapinal plant, already smoldering, and waved it under his nose. Coughing and spluttering, he inhaled the aromatic fumes. He sounded like a wine-press at full blast after harvest.

"Oh, oh, by Beng Sbodine, the Mender of Men! I am dying! My lungs burn—"

"A sip of wine, master—"

The woman in some magical way while brandishing the sprig of lapinal produced a spouted wine jug. This the man seized and upended and glug-glugged. We could see his nose was of a splendid size and proportion, a ripe glowing plum color. His whole face partook of pleasure, ripe cheeks, full lips, merry eyes, now squeezed shut as he drank. He enjoyed the good things of life, did this one.

As for the woman, fussing over him, she was not slave, for she wore a decent blue gown, with a bronze-link belt, and the comb in her long dark hair glittered. Her face held a look that might take many years to fathom, and then, when you had descried what she thought, you would be back with your first impressions of half-humorous but dedicated service to the man. And to say she fussed is to do her a disservice. She handled the man well, insuring that what he called for in the way of medicaments and wine and comfort was instantly available.

After he regained his composure, he said, "Why do I risk my health by venturing out here when the rains fall?"

He shivered. Then he said, and his voice no longer whined, "Strom Ornol, it seems you have no use for these two men, therefore I shall take them on."

The noise of the rain on the roof had not ceased all during this farcical scene. Now, in the silence after the words spoken by the man whose glowing nose was once more concealed by the yellow kerchief, the rain beat down. To a fainthearted soul that thunderous rolling barrage might well have sounded like the knell of doom.

"They are of no concern of mine, save that they must be punished for striking my servants."

Seg started to boil up at this, and I put a hand on his forearm. He lowered the bow. The yellow kerchief twitched, so the man had witnessed that little byplay.

"As they are now in my employ, I would not take kindly to their punishment by another hand."

The young lord, pale-faced rigidity personified, reacted in a way that half-surprised me. I fancied I had some, at least, of this particular relationship worked out.

"Very well, Exandu. The matter does not touch my honor. Just see they are punished."

"But, Ornol—" said the Lady Ilsa.

Strom Ornol took her arm. It was a familiar gesture.

"It is a nothing. And you should not have embroiled yourself with the lower orders. Come inside."

I bent down and helped heave Hop the Intemperate to his feet. He rubbed his chin through the hair, and winced.

"You have a fist, dom," he said.

"You have my apologies, Hop. The blow was unexpected. Otherwise you would never have—ah—fallen down."

He rubbed again and shook his head.

"As to that, I am not sure."

So, you see, somewhere along the way the world had turned and I could use the words "I apologize" to someone other than Delia. A thought worth ruminating on, that. . . .

Exandu sneezed again, and the woman went through the pantomime, and the spluttering volcano subsided. He blew his nose, hard, and sniffed, and wiped his eyes.

"Here am I like to catch my death, and all because of two rascally paktuns. Well, Hop, see to them, there's a good fellow. I must find a warm corner and a potion. Shanli! I shall need a double potion of your Special Blood Warming Lightning. As Beng Sbodine, Mender of Men, has turned his face away from me!"

"Now, now, master," soothed Shanli, taking his arm with one hand and waving the aromatic smoldering sprig of lapinal under his nose with the other, "I shall take care of you. I have a warm shirt in the oven, and Old Mother Babli's hot honey punch, with three measures of Harnafon's Forti-fied—"

"Three measures! Shanli, you do look after me. You are a treasure."

They walked off, and Hop wheezed and sniffed, and rubbed the hair over his chin, and jerked a thumb.

"Come on. If master Exandu wants to take you on, you're in luck."

We disentangled the two Gons, and helped them on their way inside. Their uniforms were of the grand style, with many dangling ribbons and straps, and, somehow, Hop wound up with a goodly length of gilt wire in his fist.

Seg laughèd.

"A boon comrade, I swear it!"

"Maybe. You'd do best to keep a watchful eye on that lord. Strom Ornol." Hop looked about. "A right nasty package, that one, due for the unraveling one fine day."

"All the same," said Seg to me as we started off along the stoop after Hop. "All the same, we strolled along here to join the expedition, not to be hired on as paktun guards."

"So we're in luck. We go along—and we get paid—"

Seg's look would have melted down the finest gold coin in all of Kregen. "You're a mercenary hulu, you really are—"

"We've both been slave, we've both been paktuns, we've both been hungry and thirsty—and we've both been fine lords. You take what comes."

"That's right, by Vox!"

"And if you can nudge fate along a litte bit—"

"All the same," said Seg, cutting in, having thought this thing through. "Fine lords, you say. We've been fine lords, and we still are! And, you're—"

"Yes. But it will surely suit our purpose better to be simple paktuns hiring out to guard this expedition? Surely?"

Seg sniffed. "Going along as minions? Very well. As you say, we take what comes."

So, into the back entrance of The Dragon's Roost we went to join up with the brave expedition venturing into the jungle-choked slopes of the Snarly Hills.

Chapter Eleven

Of Another Fist

The smells of cooking wafted deliciously from the back quarters of The Dragon's Roost. The scurry of slaves intruded an unpleasant note into an idyllic scene; but all in Opaz's good time we would remove the blot of slavery from Paz. We followed Hop the Intemperate through a room stuffed with sacks and boxes of food and hanging garlands of vegetables, and along a corridor. The kitchens lay ahead, and my mouth watered.

Hop opened the door and motioned for us to go through.

Seg went first.

I followed.

As I turned to look back for Hop an object of considerable hardness, some size, of rugged knobbyness and traveling at a goodly speed slap-bang-crashed into my chin.

I went over backwards, upsetting a pile of copper pots.

Girls started screaming. Steam filled the air. I sat up on the floor in a lake of half-cooked cabbages and stared at Hop.

He stood just inside the door, rubbing the knuckles of his right fist. He looked—through the hair—mighty pleased.

"That, I think, makes us even."

I moved my jaw. My eyes watered. I did not shake my head. My chin had click-clicked twice under each ear as I moved it.

"You, Hop the Intemperate," I said. "Have a fist, also."

"Aye."

Seg said, "It is just as well this is all friendly, for you should know, Hop the Rash, your insides would have been strewn across the floor for the cooks to inspect, had I so wished."

That, for Seg, was a long speech.

Hop chuckled.

"You are no paktuns, wandering for hire. I heard from

89

mistress Tlima but did not realize at first. You are rip-roaring lords out for adventure, and I own to some simple pleasure in feeling the tingle in my knuckles."

So that settled all our devious schemes to hire on.

We were accepted into the expedition as members. The unpleasant Strom Ornol had to acquiesce in the wishes of the majority, otherwise he would have been out of the expedition. Exandu expressed sorrow that he had not hired on two fine upstanding rogues to protect him, for, as he said between sneezes and sniffs at the aromatic fumes, and swigs of herbal and honey concoctions: "I am not long for this world. My bones are too frail to support my body, and my poor old heart strains to keep me alive. Why do I venture into so rash an undertaking?"

Privately, Hop said to Seg in a whisper, "The old fraud is after the gold and jewels, that's why."

We were introduced to the other members of the party. The spoils were to be divided into six. Seg and I now came into one share. Strom Ornol and his retinue, including the lady Ilsa, would take another. Exandu would gasp and wheeze, no doubt, while pocketing his share.

When we sat around the circular table in the window alcove corner of The Dragon's Roost, bottles and jugs nestling on the polished sturm wood, Kalu Na-Fre wrapped his tail hand around his flagon. Before lifting it to his lips, he picked up a single paline from the dish in each of his two left hands. These he popped, and chewed with relish and then the tail hand brought the flagon to his lips. With his right hand he pointed to the map, opened among the litter of bottles.

He took the flagon away and said, "The distance is not great as the fluttrell flies."

Strom Ornol, pale-faced as ever, showed his disgust.

"You are in Pandahem now, Kalu Na-Fre."

The Pachak popped two more palines with his two left hands. The right hand described circles on the map.

"My point precisely."

"It," said Exandu plaintively, "will prove a sore trial for my poor old bones."

The Pachak, Kalu Na-Fre, brushed back his long yellow hair. He used one of his left hands and his right. Before their movements were finished his right-handed tail hand lifted the flagon. These wonderful folk of Kregen with more than an apim's miserable allotment of two arms and two legs must, it is clear, be endowed with lobes in their brains that enable them to coordinate their intricate movements. As for the cunning interlocking shoulder jointing, these are marvels of bioengineering, in all the different systems found in Kildoi, Pachak, Djang and all the others.

"You do not have a suggestion, then, Kalu?"

"Only that we will have to walk once the animals can go no farther."

Exandu sniffed and consoled himself with a swig of Mother Babli's Home Brew, strongly laced, I fancied, with an expensive wine.

Kalu Na-Fre and his people would come in for their sixth share.

Any puzzlement we might have had that the booty was to be split six ways between the principals, despite the numbers of people they brought as minions, was resolved, at least in my mind, by what I surmised of the relationships here. Strom Ornol, a feckless younger son of a noble house, had been kicked out by his father to make his own way in the world. He was up past his ears in debt to Exandu.

Seg and I had put in our contribution in good Hamalian golden deldys. That currency was well-known down in the south of Pandahem, very well known. We made it crystal clear that we were not Hamalese, and backed that by our appearance as adventurers out in the world and no longer owning allegiance to any one nation.

Over in a corner the patrons of The Dragon's Roost were playing dice. The game was Soshiv and the click of the ivory cubes rattled as a background to our decisions. Soshiv—the word is one of the common ways of expressing the number eighteen—so times shiv, three times six—entails using six dice each per player. Three are thrown, the highest total being eighteen, and then the opposing players take their turns to throw against point. There are complicated betting arrangements and conventions ordering the reading of the dice. The click click and the calls as the numbers fell accompanied our deliberations as we prepared for the expedition.

Skort, the fifth member of the party, said very little. As a Clawsang he was well aware that his appearance could so unsettle and upset some people that at best they would be sick and at worst—well, Skort the Clawsang wore armor and carried weapons.

As for myself, and Seg also, as I knew, Clawsangs were merely another form of human life in the world. If you imagined that their skull-like faces, covered with a tightly stretched pebbly skin of grey and green granulated texture, blunt of jaw, the roots of the teeth exposed, the nostrils mere sunken slits, the eyes, overhung by bony projections, of a smoky crimson, if, then, you imagined this face emerging from a freshly opened grave, you could be pardoned for the thought, unworthy though it was. It was not the Clawsangs' fault they looked as though they were decomposing.

Mind you, even the stoutest hearts might flinch if they bumped into a Clawsang on a pitch-black night of Notor Zan with only the erratic illumination of a torch to pick out the rotting teeth and the decomposed nose and the glaring crimson eyes. . . .

Yet Skort was not ashamed of his appearance. Why should he be? This was the way the gods had fashioned him. Perhaps he found the jolliness of a full-fleshed ruddy countenance as offensive to him; a bloated bladder of blood.

The Clawsang's voice sounded like the rustle of bat wings from a Herrelldrin Hell as he spoke. He did so infrequently. He kept his weapons handy about him. His people maintained a sharp lookout.

Skort said, "We must march. Why do we hesitate?"

The lady Ilsa could not bear to look on Skort. Strom Ornol, over his shoulder, said, "We wait for the sorcerer."

"And if he is not here soon," said Exandu, "I shall retire to bed. I feel faint, and I am sure I have an infection in my right ear. I can hardly hear that side."

The business of the tavern went on, and ale was quaffed and the dice players threw and presently a girl came in to dance. She was a Sybli, and lusciously beautiful in a vapid way, and when she had finished a handful of copper was thrown, and one or two silver pieces. She picked them up gracefully and departed, and the ale went around again.

The local brew, made from plants tended with loving care, was a fine straw-yellow, very clear, not over strong, an ale made for quenching the thirst and not for fighting on.

Had this part of the forested area of Pandahem lent itself to hops production as I knew it, the brew would have been improved considerably. As it was, Seg and I drank a little, and talked, and sized up the people of the party with whom we would soon be risking our lives.

As Seg, speaking quietly behind his ale jug, said, "I judge the Clawsang to be a fighter, and the Pachak, clearly. This Strom Ornol could be useful if he is not wounded. Exandu?"

"He really believes he can catch all the illnesses sent by all the devils there are. But he looks healthy enough."

"Aye. And we are to have a sorcerer with us."

"If all the tales the locals tell are true, that might be not only useful but essential."

"If you believe the stories. . . ."

The inhabitants of Selsmot were riddled with the dread of the Snarly Hills. Travel toward the south went invariably all the way around in boats on the River of Bloody Jaws. The trails went east and west, for a way; not south.

The conversation, such as it was, became general as Ornol, fretfully, exclaimed, "But the bandits have stopped attacking the caravans and the river traffic. Why, then, is there still this superstitious dread of the Snarly Hills?"

The Pachak, Kalu Na-Fre, said, "Perhaps a greater evil has settled there."

The lady Ilsa looked flustered. Skort the Clawsang rubbed a skeletal hand across the rotting roots of his teeth. Ornol's color rose. And Exandu fluttered his yellow kerchief in a wild and vain attempt to halt a tremendous sneeze.

"There is a draught! I am sure of it! Shanli, my pet, find the draught—"

"Yes, yes, master. It is there, over by that window—"

She started to rise, and, in truth, a breath of air did fan in from an ill-fitting window shade. Seg stood up.

"Mistress Shanli. Please allow me."

She flushed.

Exandu, fluttering his kerchief, did not notice and Seg went across and adjusted the shade. We thought nothing of the incident.

No one spoke further on the subject of greater evils.

The risks ahead of us we could guess would be great. There is on Kregen a saying—"Don't dice with a four-armed fellow"—which attempts to caution against taking foreseeable and unnecessary risks. What we would be facing would be perils of the unknown kind.

The locals, while relishing relating to us all manner of ghastly stories of the Snarly Hills and of accepting drinks, did not wish actively to be too closely associated with us. They would not sit at our table. Their grimaces and winks, their grave nods, even the way they quaffed the ale we bought for them, all contributed to a creeping horror about to overwhelm us.

One of the locals, a Rapa, having imbibed a skinful, decided it was time to go home. His strongly vulturine face, the sharp beak surrounded by a bristle of brown and grey feathers, turned toward the door before the fellow's body followed the commands of his brain. His plain tunic was ale-stained. He was happy, though.

Tangle-footed, he swayed toward the door and then—and the transition was abrupt—he lurched sideways in terror and crashed into a table. Ale spilled. Tankards flew. The people at the table leaped back; but their protests died in their throats.

Through the open doorway came the sixth member of our party.

"At last," said Strom Ornol. "Fregeff. Now perhaps we can decide." The young lord took no notice of the turmoil the sorcerer's entrance caused.

This Fregeff, one could see at a glance, was an Adept of the Doxology of San Destinakon. Swathed in an enveloping gown of brown and black lozenges that bewildered with their subtle shifts of alignment as he moved, he presented an imposing figure simply because one knew what he was. Set against wizards of other cults, an Adept of the Doxology of San Destinakon appears dark, somber and eclipsed. This is an illusion.

Because he was a Fristle, his powerful catlike features arrogant within the hood, he did not bear a woflovol upon his left shoulder. The bronze chain about his waist connected to a bronze necklet, and that hoop rested securely around the neck of a vicious winged reptile, a volschrin, one of the rissniks. The narrow head lay low beside the Fristle's ear. A red tongue darted. The membranous wings were folded back, and the barbed tail was hidden within the sorcerer's hood. When those wings unfurled and were spread and the volschrin flew wickedly to tear out the eyes of his victim, they spanned a full arm's breadth. But his body was no larger than that of a cat, and, like his catman master, he hissed.

The hissing voice said, "Greetings and Lahal."

We all replied politely. The sorcerer moved toward our table and the empty seat. He placed his wooden-hafted bronze flail upon the sturm-wood table, and sat down. The brown and black lozenges adorning his robe shifted eye-wateringly.

No one ventured to suggest he was late for the meeting.

Fregeff turned his head and whispered to the reptile on his shoulder, and then called, "A dish of blood, and swiftly!"

Without delay a pottery dish awash in fresh chicken blood was hurried in. The serving girl, a plain-faced gentle soul, trembled as she placed the gory dish upon the table.

The volschrin hopped down, bronze links clanking, and lapped.

"Well," said Strom Ornol, his voice quivering from affronted dignity, "perhaps now we can get started."

Chapter Twelve

Through the Snarly Hills

"Hold on a moment, Seg," I said, and halted on the forest slope to catch a breath. "My lungs are on fire, and my side burns."

Seg stopped to look back. Some of the others took the opportunity to halt in a straggly line between the trees under the dim green light. Seg didn't believe me.

"It's all uphill and down my old dom, I know. But—?"

Strom Ornol bustled up. His pale face looked greenish in the light and—was that a flush of color along the cheekbones? Possible, although unlikely. . . .

"What are you lollygagging about for? Come on, come on!"

Skort the Clawsang passed me, his bulging knapsack just about finding room between me and the tree I leaned against. I had to pull back to let him pass. His skull face turned toward me, but he said nothing. Only his crimson eyes gleamed as he passed.

"Sink me!" I burst out. "I'll rupture my inward parts if we gallop along like this."

Seg's face was a picture.

The Fristle sorcerer, for whom we had waited for our meeting in The Dragon's Roost, also passed without a word. His winged pet balanced agilely on his shoulder, every now and again flirting a wing out to maintain balance. A right pair, they were. . . .

Exandu waddled up.

His face resembled Zim at the going down of the day, seen through a misty haze, embracing all around him with a roseate glow. Sweat dropped. He puffed.

"I have—" he gasped, and swallowed, and tried again. "I have a thorn through my foot. I am sure of it. And my face—I am bitten through to the bone by these pinheads!"

Shanli helped him. Her face was intent.

"I have ointments, master—when we rest—"

"When! That Ornol strides on like a madman!"

"We rest now, Exandu," I said. I turned as the blue shadow that was the lady Ilsa halted, gasping, her hand to her side. "We rest now."

"Oh," said Seg. He beamed. Then: "Why didn't you just tell the infernal idiot?"

"He believes he leads us. That is fine—" I looked away as Ilsa more fell than sat down. She still did not accept us as equals, and Seg and I couldn't care less. I said to no one in particular, "If I can't have a rest now, I will not answer for the consequences."

When Strom Ornol strode back along the line of struggling people with their burdens he found us sitting comfortably, our backs against the tree, sipping ale.

He frowned.

He picked on the lady Ilsa.

"Up, Ilsa. We must get on. You keep me waiting."

"My feet, Ornol—"

Her moccasins were strong and sensible, supple and resistant to thorns. But no one was in any doubt that marching over this forested range of hills was a laborious and painful business for anyone, let alone a girl. I had ventured, just the once, to suggest that the ladies be left in Selsmot. I had been told by Ornol to shut my mouth and keep out of his business, and by Exandu that, much as he regretted the necessity, Shanli had to go. "It's my insides, you see. Shanli understands them. She keeps me alive."

We crawled to our feet after a bit, following Ilsa, who obeyed the strom. But that was not the first or the last time I called for a halt because I was too fatigued to go farther.

Seg told Ornol, "You see, strom, he was stung by a Cabaret Plant. It has drained his strength."

"If he's this bad, he shouldn't have started."

Walking along, Hop the Intemperate said, sotto voce, "If he's this bad he'd be dead."

Seg walked with Hop for a space after that, and explained the situation. Hop's hairy face moved in an expressive way. He grasped it. Later he was seen talking to Shanli, and later still, when we stopped again, Exandu took the opportunity to say in a quiet voice, "You are a man of parts, Dray the Bogandur. A man of resource."

"I felt for your inward parts, Exandu."

"And my poor feet! And my skin, which is like Shanli's pin cushion—oh, oh, that Beng Sbodine, Mender of Men, should abandon me now!"

"Well, Exandu," said Seg in his hateful voice, "you've got the Bogandur to look after you on that score."

When we'd had a quick word to decide what names we could give these people, for they already knew we were Seg and Dray from mistress Tlima, Seg had suggested the Sublime for me. I'd riposted with the Ineffable for him.

Then I said, "How about Seg the Fearless?"

"Oh, no! Oh, no, a fellow would get into too many fights with a name like that."

"Well, if you're Naming me the Bogandur, I can but suggest the Horkandur for you, my lad."

So that was that.

We pitched camp that night and Ilsa and Exandu were not the only ones to lament their aches and pains.

A long straggly line of people stumbling through a jungle, with those in front hacking a way through when necessary, presents a prime target, but we had only a few desultory attacks from predators to ward off, and we lost only two porters. Having eaten enough food to lighten loads, we could accommodate the dead men's burdens. We carried waterproof packs on our backs, and these, we promised ourselves, would be filled with gold and gems when we returned this way.

Ha!

The reason for Seg's and my presence here was not forgotten by either of us. We even debated if, perchance, one or other of the people here in the party were agents of Spikatur Hunting Sword.

"Somebody could be," pointed out Seg. "Luring us to our doom."

"Wager?"

"We-ell . . ."

"Who do you fancy?"

"They're all runners."

"That's true, by Krun!"

Seg half glanced about as I used that Hamalese oath; no one paid us any attention. Everyone was too tired.

Everyone except Strom Ornol. From his tent the sound of singing broke discordantly on the night. A lamp gleamed through the canvas. I thought—I was not sure—a woman's shape showed, dancing.

"He likes his comforts, the strom," observed Seg.

"Aye."

"I'd mark him down. A bad egg, kicked out by his father the trylon, taken up with bad company. Anxious to hit back at the aristocratic lot who disowned him. A likely candidate for Spikatur."

"I remember a fellow, a kov, a great hunter, called Kov Loriman the Hunting Kov. He was an adherent of Spikatur. Mind you, that was in the days Spikatur struggled against Hamal and not against all and sundry."

"Well, my old dom, if we get to the place we're going, we'll find out how they changed."

"I feel that, too. But we could be mistaken."

Seg yawned. "Maybe. Just that it feels right. No, I won't back the dandy strom. Mayhap Exandu?" He yawned again.

I said, "I have the middle watch, and so I need my sleep even if you do intend to stay up all night."

In the midst of his reply Seg yawned again, and then, confound it, so did I. We turned in, to be roused out to stand our watch when the time came. At last the next day dawned in a muted green radiance dropping down through the leaves, and we could eat our breakfast and shoulder our burdens, take up our weapons and set off.

The routine of marching and resting, of fighting off predators, of arguing and surmising, and of eating and sleeping continued for a sennight as we slogged through the Snarly Hills.

We were, in truth, an oddly assorted party.

No one in his or her right mind was going to pick a quarrel with the sorcerer.

Pachaks detest quarrels as being indicative of low mental abilities and deplorable moral outlooks.

The Clawsang kept to himself and the people of his small group, and refused to be drawn into a quarrel.

Exandu turned any argument into a complaint about the state of his health, parlous, parlous in the extreme. . . .

Wanting to quarrel with any and everybody, Strom Ornol turned on Seg and me, and we, like Skort the Clawsang, refused to be drawn. We could act like onkers when we wanted to. We enraged the young strom by our obtuseness. All the same, Seg had a word with Shanli, and she had a word with Ilsa, and—by chance or not—the young dandy strom moderated his tone. Again, the hold of unpaid debts restrained him.

"The trouble is," I said, "he's holding himself in. One fine day he'll blow up."

"Let him scatter himself all over," said Seg. He spoke with a bright satisfaction. "All over."

On Kregen the image herein conjured was not that of this Earth, where an explosion means that; on Kregen the image was of a volcano blowing up. And the image pleased Seg mightily. I didn't blame my blade comrade. The truth was, Strom Ornol was well nigh insufferable. He always wanted to be in the right. He always wanted to know it all. He was, in short, a pain in the neck.

One day toward the end of the third sennight in the forest we broke through into a wide upland clearing. Water glimmered near the center, and the jungle ringed the clearing with solid dark green. We all stopped, taking our breath.

"Straight across, and skirt the lake," said Ornol.

"Well, now," started Exandu.

The strom cut him off. "If you wish to toil through the jungle, you may, fat man. As for me, I take the manly path."

Seg rolled up his eyes. I did not laugh. Ilsa came up to cling to Ornol's arm. Shanli hovered at Exandu's side. Skort stood, impassively waiting. Kalu Na-Fre looked carefully around the clearing and over the far jungle. Fregeff the sorcerer shook his bronze flail.

"The water is evil," he intoned.

To be honest, that did not surprise us.

The sense of danger scraped at our nerves.

Exandu puffed and heaved out a sigh. "My back! I ache all over! Get out the map and let us see exactly where we are."

Ornol shook out the map and we crowded around.

This famous map, we learned, started it all. From the moment it came into Exandu's possession—he was vague on the exact details, merely mumbling about red gold and slit throats—it set the fire of avarice alight. Exandu's dealings with Strom Ornol brought that young dandy in. Fregeff was known to Exandu, as was the Clawsang, Skort. The Pachak, Kalu Na-Fre, had joined them in a tavern one night when the place burned down and he had been useful in extricating a terrified Exandu. So we had joined the party, and we were all devoted to finding the treasures, and the map pointed the way.

The bandits must have amassed great treasures. They had been put down by King Crox. Alive or dead, he could be dealt with. Queen Mab, too, was missing. No news was good news. I know that Ornol envisaged walking into the bandit

lair and kicking rotting bodies aside to fling open their
treasure chests and help himself.

Fregeff shook his flail at the lake, and repeated, "The
water is evil. You may approach. I shall go the longer way."

Exandu looked longingly at the short open way, and the
dimness of the circuit. He shook his head mournfully.

"You put a poor sufferer in a great quandary. My aching
feet will never carry me all the way around; yet if we venture
across the center—"

"I am going," snapped Ornol. "I shall wait for you at the
far side of the clearing."

The map indicated four of these clearings with a central
lake. The accuracy of the map was open to question. The paper was rough, thick and coarse-grained, much tattered on
the edges, burned here and there, and with rusty brown stains
adding a decorative touch. The outlines of the river, lake and
hills were sharp enough, and the cross near the center seemed
to sit up and beg for attention. That was the lure.

The map folded up along worn creases. I wondered why
Exandu allowed Ornol to carry the precious parchment.

The strom started off, long-legged, spry, striding out over
the cleared area. He called back, harshly and imperiously:
"Ilsa!"

Instantly, the girl ran out to follow.

With some hesitations, the guards and porters followed.

The Clawsang took a fresh hitch to his belt, drew one of
his swords, gestured to his people, and followed.

The Pachak looked at Exandu.

"Go on, go on, good Kalu," wheezed Exandu. "I shall
struggle across after you. Somehow." He put out his hand
and at once Shanli was there, tall and dignified, and with his
hand on her shoulder, bitterly complaining about his poor
aching bones, Exandu waddled off.

Fregeff lowered his brozen flail. "And you?"

"I think, master sorcerer, and with no disrespect to you,
that our duty lies with the ladies and the main party."

"Then may Destinakon have you in his keeping."

Fregeff gestured to his people, and set off to edge around
the clearing.

Seg looked me in the face, half-frowning, and I nodded my
head, peaceably, and so we set off after the others.

The ground was covered with myriad gouges, like the im-
prints of a shovel, laid into the soft spongy soil. The dents

overlapped and ran in no ordered pattern. Water glimmered
in some of them. We followed along the drier parts.

At the border of the lake Ornol did not pause, but pressed
on. The water held a dank oily scum on its surface, and rainbow hues broke blisteringly from the coils. Nothing moved in
the lake; only our own onward progress changed the spec-
trum from each ridge of oily scum. The twin Suns burned
down. The air hung flat and humid. We labored on.

When we reached the far edge of the clearing and the hard
line of dark green, we stopped, and waited, and presently,
panting with the effort, Fregeff joined us.

No one—not even the usually insensitive Ornol—said anything to the sorcerer.

He said, "Why does nothing grow in the clearing?"

Before anyone got up the effort needed to think of an answer, the Fristle went on: "I will tell you. The water is evil.
It poisons the ground."

That seemed all too probable.

On that somber thought we all plunged once more into the
jungle.

Two more clearings were passed in like fashion, the party
having skirted the lake at the center waiting for Fregeff at the
far end. When we reached the fourth clearing with the heat
of the Suns declining and the green dimness in the forest
darker by contrast to the streaming mingled light out in the
open area, Seg said, "Three out of four. Good odds. But—
four out of four?"

"Fifty-fifty, I suppose, still."

"Fregeff?"

The sorcerer did not shake his flail. His cat face looked exhausted, the whiskers drooping. He was no worse off than the
others—all bar Strom Ornol.

"The evil I sensed in the waters of the other lakes is absent
here."

"So there is no problem, no hindrance," shouted Ornol.

He started off at once, over the indentations in the mud.
His figure looked hard and arrogant, lively, forceful. He led
on, and his people with the lady Ilsa followed. He half-turned
to shout back: "Come on, come on. We will camp at the far
side."

As the porters and guards moved forward, leaving the shelter of the trees and plodding on over the cleared ground, Seg
started to follow. I said, "Wait, Seg."

Fregeff turned to me.

"Why do you fear where there is no evil?"

"Why? Perhaps because you have not given your opinion?"

The Fristle sorcerer stepped out onto the mud. He was careful to step on the ridges between the indentations.

"I can tell that there is no evil in the lake. That is all."

The members of the party had by this time advanced some distance across the clearing in the waning light. We followed. The indentations, like the blows of spades, flat into the earth, appeared sharper, less eroded than in the three previous clearings. Here and there a few small green shoots showed, fragile plants growing up along the ridges between impression and impression. There had been nothing growing in the first three clearings.

Here and there, too, lay casual scatterings of bleached bones.

Seg cocked an eye at me. We loosened the swords in our scabbards, unsure, uneasy, quivering against the onset of a dread that should not exist.

As we neared the water we could see the surface was crystal clear and sparkling where it was not covered by broad lily pads, blue-green and velvet with lushness in the low-lying light.

Strom Ornol strode on. At his side the lady Ilsa struggled bravely to keep up. The porters bent under their loads. The guards looked about, white of eye, and their heads turned this way and that as though under imminent attack from the air. The Pachak openly drew his swords. The Clawsang copied him. A sweet and intrusive scent gusted from the lake. The lily pads floated silently.

When I spoke to the sorcerer, my voice was hushed.

"No evil, Fregeff?"

"No evil of a supernatural kind that I can tell."

"There is *something* wrong with this place." Seg pulled his bow off his shoulder, the stave lay clenched in his left hand. He lifted his right to draw an arrow—and the surface of the lake boiled.

Lily pads swirled wildly away. From the sparkling water enormously long stems flailed. Dozens of them, bunched and thrashing, they heaved from the water, scattering glinting drops, slashed frenziedly at the members of the party.

At the tip of each flailing stem a bloated flowerlike object smashed down, hard, splitting into the earth, splashing mud in gouts, leaving spadelike indentations.

A Gon guard was smashed into jelly.

The people screamed. They were running, some fell and were squashed. Blood oozed into the mud. The hammer-hard flower heads flailed at us, lashed down, smashed into the earth with soggy deadly smacks, driving deep gouges into the mud.

I drew my sword and, raving, leaped forward.

Chapter Thirteen

Concerning a Distortion of Reality

Seg leaped alongside, bow thrust back over his shoulder, sword in fist. We burst past Fregeff, who was looping up his bronze chain around the little shoulder-perching reptile. His bronze flail clashed.

Shoulder to shoulder, Seg and I drove forward into the flailing forest of lashing stems. The platelike mangling flower heads swung with tremendous force. The stink of disturbed mud filled our nostrils, till we gagged.

With ferocious slashes, we cut and hacked at the stems as they swooped near. They were sinewy, not easy to hack through, and from the gashes opened by our swords a thick and slimy brown ooze dribbled.

The screams of the terrified people racketed on never-endingly. Through the whirlwind of stems and the looping darting rock-hard flower-heads we glimpsed Strom Ornol, hacking and slashing. The other members of the party fought back. The porters reacted differently, each according to his race. Some dropped to their knees to pray and were so squashed into the mud. Others put their heads down and ran. Others hefted their bundle or bale and tried to beat off the terrible plants. Most of these, too, were squashed.

Seg pelted on before me, incensed, head up, his sword blurring. He lopped a plant stem clean through, catching it near the head where it was thinner and more tender. He scooped up Shanli in his left arm. He made loud squelching noises as he ran.

Following on as fast as I could I saw Ornol flailing away, and the lady Ilsa hanging to his left arm, hampering him and yet gaining protection from her nearness. She, I judged, would be safer with Ornol than if I attempted to snatch her. Ornol would as lief take a swipe at me, a suddenly appearing attacker in the corner of his eye, as at a plant.

Sword flailing above my head in ghastly parody of the plant stems flailing at us, I ranged up alongside Seg and Shanli. Exandu was just about done for. His face bloated scarlet. His eyes stood out. Yet he was bashing away with a heavy curved single-edged sword. He used it with a cunning skill, and all the time he bashed at the plant stems, he was maintaining a high-pitched catalog of all the complaints besieging his poor abused body.

"Aid me, Dray the Bogandur! Help a poor old fellow who—"

"You appear to be doing well enough," I shouted, sliding and almost going over. "I'll stay with you. Run!"

Then a damned hard-edged flower whistled down at my head. It was useless to stand up to them and cut through the stem. If you did that the head would simply fly straight on and bash you. You had to duck and weave and slash cunningly, avoiding the blows.

"They can't see us!" bellowed Seg. "Yet they strike with uncanny accuracy."

"Magic," said Shanli, under Seg's arm. "It is sorcerers' work."

Puffing and bloated, Exandu slashed along with a will with companions to protect his side.

"No magic—Shanli, my treasure. They strike at noise."

I had to say it, for I was annoyed with myself.

"There is no noise of bottles and glasses, or of people having a good time. It seems these things have no need of enticing us."

"We were—fool enough—to come near them."

The terror and confusion persisted. We had a long way to go. The impressions of the murderous flower heads reached everywhere in the clearing. There was no safety until we reached the hostile jungle.

We lost good men. Mere squashed red puddles, they had to be left as we fought to escape. Even the bundles they carried had to be left. Swishing our swords, taking more care to strike exactly, leaving a trail of decapitated flower heads, we labored on toward the far side of the clearing, for that was the nearest now. I thought to glance back.

The Fristle sorcerer stood stock still. The volschrin clung like a scaled polished statue. His hood was thrown back. His strong cat face was upturned. He did not move; he made no sound—and the devilish killer plants ignored him.

I gasped for a breath.

"Exandu! Stand still. Do not move, do not make a sound."

When he understood, he stopped running. His body shook. Sweat ran thickly down his cheeks. Seg stopped, too, grasping Shanli. We all stood, swords poised, staring about, using our sight, the weapon we had that could trump the killer plants.

The stems wreathed and writhed above our heads, the blind flowers seeking prey. Those stems flailing and lashing at our party continued to do so. We breathed short, watching as more men were felled into red puddles. The stems left us alone. We breathed easier, getting our breath—

And Exandu sneezed.

Instantly two plant heads uncoiled and swished down at the source of the sound.

Seg chopped one, and I chopped the other.

He raised his eyebrows at me. I knew what he meant.

"By the Veiled Froyvil, my old dom!" he was saying silently. "How long are we to stand here like a couple of loons?"

I didn't know. Once Exandu got his breath back—we'd run. Our squelching progress through the muck would alert the killer plants, and down they would swoop.

Fregeff lifted his flail. He lifted the bronze links silently. He looked proud, defiant, the recipient of powers that would blast a lesser man. The whiskers of his catlike face bristled.

He shook the flail.

Above the diminishing screams of the running people and the ghastly swishing sounds made by the killer plants, we in our pool of petrified silence heard the bronzen links of the flail clash together.

Rearing from the crystal waters of the lake, pushing the velvet lily pads aside, swooping out at any sound to smash their victims flat, the pallid stems swayed toward Fregeff. The wizard shook the flail again.

The blind flower heads above him, their edges hard and square, drew back. They wilted. They writhed, and now they writhed as though caught in an open flame. Swiftly, they withdrew, coiled, disappeared beneath the waters of the lake. It was as if, through the agency of his flail the wizard had told them to turn tail, yield, flee. . . .

Again the sorcerer shook the flail of the Scourging of San Destinakon.

The chiming sounded sweetly in our ears, yet, in all truth, it was a sound of utmost horror.

The wizard emitted no brilliant gust of flame and fire, no

bolt of lightning, such as the incandescent bolts with which
the sorcerer's Quern of Gramarye was formed. And we knew
the power came not only from Fregeff and not only from the
flail; the thaumaturgy boiled from the conjunction of the two.
Invisibly, the power smote a circle of clarity among the
swooping pallid killer plants.

Exandu shook himself. He whispered, and he thought he
whispered only to himself; but we heard, Seg and I, we
heard.

"To Opaz the Nine times Exalted, who has the mastery
over all men, be the praise!"

Under my blade comrade's arm Shanli erupted into a violent squirming bundle of womanliness. "And, Pantor Seg the
Horkandur! If you would put me down, I shall be about my
work!" Her voice was loud, strong, not shrill but overpowering. I understood she spoke and acted thus to cover up the
words spoken by Exandu.

Seg stood her up. She did, in that moment, look magnificent. Instantly, she was ministering to Exandu, fiddling
with his straps and clothes to put him to rights, soothing his
brow, producing a bottle of a honey-gold liquid, which gave
him something to stop his querulous complaints.

Seg smiled.

Fregeff joined us, still remote, wrapped in the aura of
power. We did not shrink away as we had every right to do;
but we were conscious of the dark authority of the man. In
the normal course of events I give wizards a wide berth. I
count some sorcerers as good friends. Fregeff, a Fristle, a
cat-man, might yet number among those. That lay with the
gods.

"We give you thanks, San Fregeff."

He inclined that cat head, and with the links of the flail
brushed his whiskers. Before replying he whispered to the
volschrin perched on his shoulder. The reptile flicked his
wings. Fregeff addressed the volschrin as Rik Razortooth.
Spreading his membranous wings, the reptile flapped away
and sailed toward the nearest severed flower head, trailing his
thin bronze chain. He settled and began to rip at the hard
carapace of the flower head.

Fregeff said, "I was right when I said there was no evil
in the water. The evil in the other lakes had killed the plants.
Whoever placed that evil there knew what he or she was doing."

Skort the Clawsang marched back over the mud toward us.

Fregeff went on: "But I own I was slow. We have lost porters and guards. I shall abase myself to San Destinakon this night, and chastise myself in expiation."

"Nonsense, San," said Skort. His ghastly face leered upon us, the ruby eyes slits of smoldering anger. "The fault was ours. You have saved us all."

I said, "You have met these plants before?"

"Aye. Slaptras. They grow in Chem, along with syatras and tenchlas."

"Everything happened very quickly after the plants attacked," pointed out Seg in his superior and endearing way, knowing exactly what he was doing. "I think Skort is right and San Destinakon has no need of a scourged back this night."

"As to that, Horkandur, I can only say my business is my business. I have no need of sermons from others."

I felt the chill.

Exandu, blustering, blowing, sneezing, moaning pitifully and bellowing angrily, broke in. He did not relish, as I saw it, the loss of the limelight. I was wrong in that. . . .

"Let us leave this infernal place and schtump! The spell may not last long enough for my poor aching feet to carry me into that terrible jungle away from the slaptras."

Fregeff gave the bronze chain a single jerk, and the volschrin flew back to his shoulder. Ruby eyes regarded us. "It was hardly a spell," said the sorcerer. "More a distortion of reality—well, my business is my business."

We all made our way across the mud to the trees. The bodies and the bundles would be taken care of. We made camp and more than one of us wondered if the future held more horrors. Most of us were faithfully convinced that the future *did* hold more horrors. . . .

Our faith was justified.

Chapter Fourteen

I Receive a Personal Invitation

On Earth, I am informed, the tropical rain forests occupy less than ten percent of the land surface of the planet, yet they contain half of the species of the world. Whether this be so or not, in view of the claims of the sea, is beside the point; the truth remains, tropical rain forests are wonderful, mysterious secret worlds of their own, romantic, pulsating with drama, hot and sticky and uncomfortable and downright dangerous.

Seg and I had no retainers, and we hadn't bothered with a tent or beds or tables and chairs, as the others had. We camped as we had camped on many a night and many a place of Kregen. We were old campaigners.

From the canopy above where the leaves spread out into jigsaw patterns between branch and branch and tree to tree, down to the soft ground where the detritus piled up, and was consumed and carried away, each level contained its own slice of life. We did not venture into climbing. We toiled along the floor, wending a way between massive vine-covered trunks. When we camped at night we formed the tents into a circle and set fires and watches. More often than not we were disturbed; but we had some handy fighters with us, and we were more than a match for the denizens of the jungle.

At least, for some of them. . . .

On the last night before the map told us we would reach the upper lake and the waterfall and the rocky cliff, Seg and I passed a few words about our companions. What those words boiled down to, essentially, was: We didn't know.

"Kalu the Pachak will, like Pachaks, be an honorable man. I am surprised he is mixed up with a rogue like Ornol, or that shuddery fellow, Skort——"

"I," I said, "have Exandu picked for a villain."

110

"We-ell, you could be right. He is reticent about his trade. And he did pray to Opaz the Nine Times Exalted."

"Which marks him as not being a Pandeheem."

"Unless he's been converted." And Seg laughed.

Usually new lands are visited by the Four M's. The Military, the Merchants, the Mercenaries, and the Missionaries.

"We had some sprightly dealings with the missionaries of the Black Feathers of the Great Chyyan," I said, "and it is sure Skort the Clawsang worships dark gods. But Exandu?"

"Tomorrow we fetch up with the drikingers' lair. We'll find out more then." Seg rolled over in his bag. "G'night."

And, all in good time, on the morrow we marched up to the edge of the forest and looked out across the lake toward the sheer face of rock.

Everyone, instinctively, checked the water first for signs of slapras. We saw no velvety blue-green lily pads.

Storm Ornol said, "I march around to the right."

Exandu puffed and said. "The way to the left seems shorter."

Skort the Clawsang half drew and then thrust back his sword into the scabbard. This sword was a lynxter, which is a Lohvian sword, something like the Havilfarese thraxter. Skort knew about the jungles of Chem, which is in Loh. But he had not vouchsafed any information of his origins. Like the rest of them, he was reticent on the point, and we were happy to take them all, like us, as plain adventurers.

"I think I will go with Strom Ornol," said Skort.

The lake shimmered in the mingled radiance of the Suns of Scorpio. The jungle pressed in around the perimeter. Directly opposite us the wall of rock towered, smothered in vines, brilliant with flowers. Many birds swooped and called one to the other, cavorting in midair. There seemed, at first glance, little to choose which way we went. The heat shimmered off the lake, and the rock face wavered in heat distortions.

Among the birds flying and disporting I saw—suddenly and quick—a magnificent golden and scarlet bird. He flew up out of the entangling vines, and circled around the edge of the lake. I watched him narrowly, my companions forgotten.

He swerved. In headlong flight he soared straight above my head, wide winged, glorious, the light of the suns incandescent upon his feathers. He was the Gdoinye, the spy and messenger of the Everoinye, the Star Lords.

Among the people clustered at the edge of the forest, I knew only I, of them all, could see the Gdoinye.

He cawed, arrogantly, and banked, wide-winged, magnificent of plumage, and soared away around the right-hand side of the water.

I said, "Master Exandu, I think the right-hand way will be easier on your fragile bones."

His flushed face jerked up, and sweat dropped off the end of his roseate nose.

"You think so?"

"Aye."

"Well, perhaps—you, San Fregeff. What do you think?"

"I will go with Strom Ornol."

The Pachak, Kalu, answered the unspoken question by starting off. He turned to his side where he had one arm only.

Everybody followed.

The distant roar of the waterfall indicated its presence; we could not see it yet. The powerful scent of flowers stung my nostrils. I cocked a wary eye at Seg.

"Yes. Spiny Ribcrushers."

"I fancy Skort will know of them."

We picked out way with great caution around the edge of the lake. Roots of trees snaked into the water. We watched everything with the care of men who have marched through a jungle.

On the brown mudspit the birds quarreled. The brown water shimmered with heat. We kept our weapons in our fists, and we plodded on until we circumnavigated the right half of the lake and so stood before the first of the rocky buttresses.

The lianas twined away above, looping and jumbled, coiling into massy knots and protuberances. The rock dripped with moisture, grey and leprous. The weatherbeaten appearance was occasioned by an intricate and enormously extended series of carvings. Faces, birds, fish, animals, risslacas, insects, grotesque and beautiful, the carvings swarmed upon the rock and in the heat shimmer appeared to move and breathe with a pseudo life, at once fascinating and disturbing.

Exandu stopped and wiped his face. Skort moved on, around the end of the buttress. Strom Ornol, at the Clawsang's side, half-turned back and motioned us on.

"There is an opening, a portal."

The sight of the gorgeous bird sent by the Star Lords had, as so often in the past it had not, reassured me. Oh, yes, the Everoinye liked to keep an eye on me from time to time; perhaps in this instance that was all they were doing. Very probably that was the true answer. But, was it not a human weakness to try to see the Gdoinye's actions, flying around the right hand side of the lake, as some kind of assistance?

We all shuffled around the buttress and saw the opening in the rock, square, hard, forbidding.

Seg whispered, "If there are bandits around, are we to go strolling in like players at feast time?"

"I gather Exandu and Ornol believe they will encounter only dead men, and can help themselves to the treasures."

"That's as may be."

The square opening was twice man height, and three times man wide, and the architrave was surrounded by grotesque gargoylish carvings, obscene monstrosities sculpted by a depraved master hand. Inscriptions, etched into the rock, proclaimed the standard curses. Because many of the artisans employed on masonry work were unable to read or write, either the literate master mason would chalk out the words, and the hammer and chisel men would faithfully follow his outlines, or a stencil would be placed on the stone and fuming acid poured on to etch out the words. We all stared at the ritual curses.

Not one of these hardy adventurers would be affected by the blastings and ib-destructions and diseases promised for anyone who entered here. They were accustomed, in the adventurer's trade, to weightier obstacles than mere carven words.

Then Exandu let out a quick, chopped-off cry of alarm. Kalu said, "That is indeed strange." Skort said nothing and Ornol shouted for his people to prepare torches.

Fregeff the wizard pulled his hood up over his head, and he covered his volschrin, Rik Razortooth, with the hood.

I turned back from examining a marvelously carved head of a Medusa to hear Seg say, "By the Veiled Froyvil! I don't believe it!"

So I turned around and saw Seg standing, mouth open, finger pointing, staring in horror at the blasphemous inscriptions.

Three lines of writing in the flowing Kregish script, all beauty and curve and free-flowing line, had been blasted into the rock. They looked black, as though some instrument dispensing enormous heat had simply burned the stone away.

Three lines of writing, and the center line was a mere nothing, a repetition of the rote curses;

ENTER TO YOUR DOOM

Well, one ignored that. But I looked, standing beside Seg, and I saw. . . . I saw! The first line of writing said:

DRAY PRESCOT, EMPEROR OF VALLIA

And the last line of writing said:

PHU-SI-YANTONG

The heavens did not open and darkness did not descend on my senses. But it was a near thing, by Vox!

All manner of impossible thoughts clashed and collided in my brain. Phu-Si-Yantong, that arch-devil, the Wizard of Loh who had brought great misery to the people of many lands, and particularly to those of Vallia and Pandahem, was dead. He was dead. He had been blown away in a supernal gout of fire in the Quern of Gramarye, in the Jikhorkdun in Ruathytu. He was dead. How could he have known, so long ago, that I would visit here? Could he have sent his ib in lupu into the future?

Seg took my arm.

"He's dead."

"Yes."

"Horkandur?" said Shanli's gentle voice. "Pantor Seg—you are feeling ill?"

Seg swallowed.

"I am all right, thank you, mistress Shanli. Perhaps the smell of the Spiny Ribcrushers affects me."

We smiled at Shanli. We made ourselves smile for her. She did not flinch back.

"They do have an—an overpowering smell, true. The strom insists on going first. Would you—may I ask—pantors . . ."

I said, "We will stay with you and Exandu, Shanli."

"My thanks, my lord."

The macabre message, weird, eerie, of another time, had to be pushed away. Yantong was dead and burned to pieces. We were here, chasing the remnants of the followers of Spikatur Hunting Sword. Our task was not finished. Useless to fret over the hows of the message blasted into the rock. Its black-burned letters remained; no one commented on them. Once you've read one ceremonial curse you've read them all. Perhaps the others couldn't see the message, as though it had been blasted out for Seg's and my eyes alone. I hesitated no longer. Shouldering my bundle, my sword in my right hand, I followed on as Exandu's people, carrying torches, plunged into the darkness beyond the portal.

They did not make a great deal of noise; but the sound of moccasins shuffled hushed on the ancient stones, the clink of armored men rang with a subdued tone, the harsh breathing stifled. We walked on, into a chamber cut from the rock. Our lights revealed two doors at the far end, both closed, and I surmised we were in for more argument over choosing the way.

Strom Ornol said, "Right."

Still mazed by the message from a dead foeman—or foe-sorcerer—I couldn't have cared less which was selected. We had to find Pancresta and her friends, and see what we could do to remove the new evil of Spikatur Hunting Sword. Seg and I followed through the right-hand door.

Slaves went past carrying long poles cut from the forest. Seg glanced at the poles and frowned. He spoke to a Rapa slave as the fellow passed.

"How long is that pole?"

The Rapa's beaked face ducked. "Ten feet, master."

"H'm," said Seg, as we all walked quietly down a stone corridor. "We shall need a few bundles of those, I shouldn't wonder."

"Aye," I said. "Remarkably useful items."

Kalu, an adventurer well-versed in enterprises of this nature, said, "Where I come from, we often talk of going ten-foot poling." He did not say where he came from. "And of green-sliming. I think we should march together."

"You've done this before, then, Kalu." Seg made it a statement.

"Yes. It is a living."

I said, "So your tavern meeting with the good Exandu was not by chance." Then I laughed, letting Kalu see the laugh was all good natured. "Mayhap the fire . . . ?"

He shook his head and his wild Pachak hair flared yellow. "No. I would not stoop to that. And, were our position other than it is, Bogandur, I might needs challenge you."

We walked through the right-hand doorway and followed the party, the leaders of whom prodded the floor assiduously.

"You could, Kalu. But I would not fight you over so important a matter. I respect the honor of Pachaks too highly."

Someone up front let out a yell and we crowded on to enter a chamber, robed in black, lit by fire crystal in the roof above, and with a vast and circular stairway leading down positioned at the center. Here was a problem.

"There is no other way forward," said Ornol. "So we go down."

The stairs were broad, hewn from rock, slippery. There was no handrail. The depths below resounded with blackness.

"My heart and lungs," said Exandu. He gasped. "This will do my rheumatics no good at all."

"When we rest, master," said Shanli, "I will poultice your joints with Mother Rashi's Herbal Attachments."

"Oh, yes, Shanli. They always ease the stiffness."

Seg and Kalu exchanged a smile, and we all descended the winding stairs into the depths.

Three-quarters of the way down, with the darkness at the foot of the stairs lightening to the glow of the torches, Skort the Clawsang waited on the steps. He stood bravely enough on the outside as the people walked down against the wall. When we came up with him, with Seg and Kalu still talking together, Skort's hideous decomposing corpse face leered on us.

"The strom bids silence from this point down."

Kalu started to bristle up, but Seg, amicably, said, "That makes sense, good Skort."

From the way my blade companion spoke, I knew he was not plucking feathers, as they say on Kregen. Of course, silence made sense down here. We went on, quietly, and the oppressive stillness of the place began its insidious work on our nerves.

The spiral stairway gave onto a flat expanse of rock, with an opening ahead of us and another to our right. The left-hand side of the expanse was walled off solidly. There were no doors in the two openings. A warrior moved forward with a pole and prodding the floor, prodded past the central opening.

He was a Chulik, with tusks unadorned, and a blue-dyed pigtail. He turned and motioned us. All was well.

Chuliks, trained from birth to be mercenary warriors, may have nothing much of warm humanity in their makeup; they are superb fighters and they are brave, you have to say that of them. This Chulik served Strom Ornol.

We all followed on through the opening and found we had to turn sharply to the left along a fifteen-foot-wide corridor. The walls were solid rock. The ceiling and floor were rock. Our torches flung shards of light along, and the procession of heads cast grotesque shadows ahead of us.

No rooms opened off the corridor. At the far end the pasages turned ninety degrees to the right. Halfway along another opening showed merely blackness to the questing torches. Strom Ornol marched straight past this opening and went with his people around the far corner.

When Kalu reached the corner he used his sword to mark a sign upon the rocky wall.

In one sense he needn't have bothered. Every corner was lavishly inscribed with marks. Numbers, letters, names, exhortations, they crowded the rock as the light from the torches fell across them. Seg nodded at this display of ancient instant cartography.

The Pachak leaned close, whispering, "I have a system."

All I did was to make note of the sign which, by reason of its semi-obliteration of others beneath it, indicated it to be among the most recent additions. This mark was in the form of a heart, lobed, and as we passed various corners I noted that the slashed line through the heart pointed the way we had come.

On we went. Because Ornol insisted on leading us, and Skort stuck with him, and Fregeff shuffled along after, Exandu and Kalu and Seg and me tended to be always bringing up the rear. This seemed a sensible idea. Danger, when it came, could strike from our back as easily—possibly more easily—than from our front.

The onward progression of our party, which, despite the losses we had suffered battling through the jungle and at the Pool of the Slaptras, was still of some size, created enough noise for the prohibiton upon conversation to be relaxed. Although I accepted this, I did so with reservations. Kalu, who knew about these things, was cheerful enough as he told us, "Oh, yes. The guardians of the tombs usually know if folk come adventuring down. We will know when we have found them well enough. Yes, by Papachak the All-Powerful!"

"But we're not delving down tombs!" protested Seg.

Kalu waved his upper left arm, shield slung over his back. "What's the difference? Down here?"

We went on following the leaders until we reached an echoing chamber, vaulted of rocky ceiling, lit by ghostly fires that sent streamers of light disturbingly across the floor. The whole system of rooms and corridors was free of dust. This made me suspicious. In this chamber there were twelve doors, set around the circumference. I noticed the mark of the heart upon the door we entered. Halfway around the chamber lay the corpses of two werstings and two strigicaws, savage hunting beasts, long of fang and claw. The bodies appeared to be mummified. All four throats had been slit.

On the other side, propped against a wall, sat the corpse of a man. He, too, was mummified. He was a Chulik. He had been powerful, and wore scraps of armor. His weapons had been taken from him. Farther along lay a scattering of bones, and the skulls of two Rapas and a Fristle.

"They make you welcome," observed Kalu. He sounded quite cheerful, perfectly at home. But he gazed about alertly, and his group of Pachaks closed up, watchfully.

Just as we were about to follow Strom Ornol through one of the doorways without knowing why he had chosen this particular one, we all stopped, poised. The sound of screaming reached us. The black-paneled door to our left crashed open. A man staggered through. He was a Pachak. His lower left arm was a mere stump, bandage-swathed. He was clad in tatters. He carried a sword, rusty with blood. His Pachak face showed such terror as made the heart leap in shocked sympathy.

He sprang out onto the rocky floor, and swung about, flinging the sword up before his face.

Out from the door after him leaped the forms of fanged nightmares, feral eyes ablaze, razored talons reaching to rip past his feeble defense and tear his head from his shoulders.

Amid the instant pandemonium that shattered about us I saw the bristle hairs of the hellhounds spiking in ungovernable anger. They yowled in frenzy, foam-spitting, their red tongues lolling between those razor teeth.

In the next second the hellhounds leaped, lethal engines of destruction, charged demoniacally full upon us.

Chapter Fifteen

In the Maze

Seg loosed and in the same motion he dragged his sword clear of the scabbard. Kalu's shield slapped across in his two left hands, and his right brought the sword up, his tail hand whistling over his head, curved blade glittering. My own sword joined in and we fronted that first crazed charge.

Exandu moaned and drew his single-edged sword and stood with us. Slaves screamed and ran. The warriors of the party stood, back to back, in clumps, or with their backs against the wall. The noise echoed in a racket of snarls and shrieks, of muffled chomping of sharp fangs and the juicy thwunk of blows. Keen steel drew bright red blood.

We fought the hellhounds.

We strewed their bristly lean bodies over the rocky floor, trailing blood. We slashed and hacked at them, and they yowled and snarled, and kept coming, a tide of hairy wolflike bodies pouring through the black-paneled doorway.

They took their toll of our people.

Striking like a maniac, I tried to keep Exandu and Shanli covered, and Seg ranged up on the other side. We had no shields; but we skipped and pumped and ducked. Our brands stained gory, and the blood splashed up to our shoulders.

At last, at last it was done, and no more hairy hellhounds, teeth ravenous, eyes crazed, leaped for our throats. The black-paneled doorway gaped—empty.

"Now may Beng Sbodine, the Mender of Men, have us in his mercy." Exandu spoke deliberately. He shook blood drops from his sword. Seg glanced at me. We marked Exandu's mode of speech. Nothing here, then, of Opaz the Nine Times Exalted.

Strom Ornol, blood-splashed, kicked the hairy and bloodied corpse of a hellhound. He bent, picked the thing up, and threw it viciously from him.

119

"Creatures from hell!" His pallor was intense.

"They are mortal, not supernatural," said Fregeff.

At his feet lay four hellhounds, unmarked, but dead, stone dead.

Shanli started to minister to Exandu. Skort bent to one of his retainers. The decomposed appearance of the man was a gruesome reminder that soon he would no longer belie his looks.

"Poor Sangl," said Skort. "How am I to tell his mother of this?"

Others of our party were down; a shaven-headed Gon, an uncouth Brokelsh, a Fristle who served Fregeff. No Pachaks had been lost. Kalu knew his own men well.

"We must push on." Ornol waved his sword commandingly, and blood drops splattered. "Ilsa—you must march."

The girl stood up, trembling, from where she had crouched in the angle of floor and wall. She bore dark smudges beneath her eyes, and the tears coursed down her cheeks.

"Yes, Ornol, yes. Those poor men—those terrible beasts—"

"They can be slain with steel." Ornol waved his sword and strode off, commandingly. We all followed.

Seg shouted. "We can't just leave our own people like this!"

Ornol half-turned.

"Can you bury them in this rock? Do you wish to carry them with you?"

Seg looked furious. I walked over to the Gon and, bending down, gently removed the shield that he had failed to employ properly and so save his life. "At least," I said, "we can say the proper words over them and commend them to their gods, and then take from them what in brotherly comradeship they no longer need and we do."

This, with due solemnity, we did.

These small rites meant that Seg and I were last to leave the chamber, with Kalu and Exandu just ahead.

When in the town of Selsmot mistress Tlima had sent a slave over to The Dragon's Roost with our belongings, we had resumed possession of our equipment and weapons. Our own clothes, being mere rags, we did not bother with, and continued to wear the brown tunics. I own I felt the usual irrational but understandable longing to be wearing the brave old scarlet.

"Good men are dead," I said. "I fancy there will be more before we find Pancresta."

"Aye," said Seg. "And before we get out of this devilish place."

"Well, by Zair!" I said with some force. "Just make sure, Horkandur, that you are not one of them!"

"And you—Bogandur!"

With a suspicious look back, we went on. "And that poor devil of a Pachak. Who was he? Where did he come from?"

We assumed that, as he was a Pachak, he would not be a bandit.

Fresh shouts up ahead hastened our steps, and we arrived in the next chamber to find Strom Ornol and Exandu locked in mulish argument. This room, lit by the pervasive glow of fire-crystal walls, gave off a pungent reek of rotting flesh. A small pool of water at the center, rock-coped, held a miniature slaptra. The thing was slashing about with hard-edged flower heads at the end of stalks some two meters long.

Exandu and Ornol might argue over which door to take next; a goodly number of the folk were standing laughing at the slaptra. They taunted it as though it could understand. A Gon stepped forward, and slashed with his sword. The flower head flew off. They all laughed again.

As though that was the signal, the warriors leaped on the slaptra and hewed it to pieces.

No doubt they felt better after that.

"Very well, master Exandu! Very well. You may come with me, as you wish. I go through the door marked in green."

"But, strom—"

"I shall go with you, Strom Ornol," cut in Skort.

"And I," said the wizard.

When the whole mob advanced on the green door, busily poking the ground ahead of them with their poles, and casting searching glances over their heads, Seg and I, with Kalu, saw no reason why we should not follow along.

Green doors, blue doors, black doors, they were all one.

Three long corridors later, and two rooms containing, one: skeletons piled up in yellow-brown heaps, and, two: rotting wooden chests spilling dust and moths, we came to a blue-paneled door. This the leaders pushed open. At once shouts of dismay echoed down to us in the rearguard.

We pushed along and entered the next chamber, weapons ready for what might leap upon us.

We saw a large circular room, halfway around which lay the corpses of two strigicaws and two werstings. Opposite

them sat the corpse of a Chulik. Bones lay scattered near.
And by the black-paneled door a heap of still blood-reeking
hellhound corpses, and those of men, lay in a shambles.

The variety of oaths that rose was marvelous in its diver-
sity.

"Twelve doors!" shouted Ornol above the din, pressing
them down by the pallid force of his face and authority. "We
have nine left. Let us take the yellow door."

Yellow seemed a sound enough choice to me. I glanced at
the red door. It would not be as easy as that. . . .

By the time we had traced a weary way through rooms
and corridors, and reentered the circular room through the
orange door, we had rested once, and were still tired and
more than dispirited. Exandu was one long moan. Ilsa
plumped down, and put her hands to her face, and wept
openly.

"The turquoise door!" cried Ornol. "Follow me."

His warriors dragged themselves up from whence they had
flopped down, and kicked the slave porters into motion, and
obediently started after Ornol. Skort the Clawsang and his
people followed. Ornol swung back, his pale face wrathful.

"Ilsa! Where are you?"

I went up to Ornol. My face was perfectly blank.

"Strom. It is needful that we rest."

He sneered at me. "Strom, is it? Is that the way to address
me? You call me pantor—"

"Pantor. We rest now. You may go on; but you will go on
alone."

He glared about. Exandu tried to rescue the situation, for
it was obvious and petty enough, Zair knows.

"A rest, good Ornol, for longer than the ten murs you allowed us in the room of the hanging virgins. I beg you."

I said, "We camp here. Set the guards and let us brew
some tea and cook ourselves a meal. Our rations will stand
that—"

"Our rations and water are almost gone," said Kalu.

"Aye. We must keep up our strength if we are to escape,"
said Exandu.

"Escape? We have not yet started!" burst out Skort.

We all stared at him in astonishment. As though alarmed
at the vehemence of his outburst, he went off, his corpse face
seeming to deliquesce and melt away to teeth and bone, and
started bellowing at his people to make camp.

We made camp and set watches and tried to sleep. This

place of tunnels and rooms was beginning to become a trial. It reminded me uncomfortably of the Moder I'd been down in Moderdrin, the Humped Land, although—as yet—in nowise as horrifying. And this puzzled me, for I, along with the others, had been set for a trial of strength with the bandits, if they were not all dead. This maze came as a shock.

"Seems to me, my old dom, as though we shall all starve to death."

"I could eat hellhound, if I had to. So could you."

"Aye, and so could the others, if it came to it. They'd drink hellhound blood, too. . . ."

"If Zair wills it."

When we started up again after a camp of some eight burs or so, we rose with much groaning and clicking of joints, and the slaves had to be kicked into motion by equally sore warrior guards. We all straggled off, poking the floor and watching the ceiling, and followed Ornol through the doorway paneled in turquoise.

We had not eaten to break our fast, determining to press on for a few burs before consuming any more of our fast vanishing rations. We entered the next chamber, one of three, at the branch of the corridor. Everyone exclaimed in surprise.

Down two sides of the room, which was clothed in bright tapestries depicting scenes of the hunt, stood two long tables. White damask shone. The service was of silver and the viands smelled so aromatic that the saliva started up in our mouths. Amphorae of wine stood in their tripods racked against the far wall. The place was set for a feast.

Kalu swung to us. "Let no one eat or drink!"

The rush for the tables halted, suddenly. We stared longingly on the viands. Our mouths were parched and our tongues hung out. Ornol clamped his lips. He pointed at a slave, a Brukaj with a stubborn bulldog face. "You! Sit at the table and eat, drink!"

"Master!" quavered the Brukaj, shaking.

Ornol lifted his sword. He placed the point against the slave's neck, under his ear. He twitched. A thread of blood shone. "Eat, drink! Or die!"

Ilsa hurried forward; but Shanli was there, to hold her. Exandu sat down on one of the chairs. Everyone else watched. I watched, for I felt, suddenly, that this place was not as the Moder had been.

The slave ate and drank, quivering with fear. But the food was marvelous, delicious, and the wines superb. Soon he was sweating with enjoyment, and drinking—and singing. He sang merrily, throwing his arms about, his lowering bulldog face transformed.

"If he dies, he'll die happy," said Exandu, with a sigh.

"If the poison does not torture him too much," said Seg, a savage note in his voice. Fierce and fiery is my comrade Seg, with a heart as soft as a girl's lips—at times.

"We will sit and wait," said Ornol.

I fancied he had not liked the hint of mutiny. This hiatus gave him the chance to allow us a proper rest. If the slave died—but the Brukaj did not die. We fell on the food and drink, and, by Krun it was good, all of it, superb!

At last, stuffing our packs with food and carrying bottles of wine, we set off again.

After a long march in the lambent glow of the fire-crystal walls, a march wherein we met and bested fearsome Bearded Phantoms, whining Mind Leeches and a covey of stinking Dragworms, we returned to the chamber, one of three, where we had feasted.

Our exclamations of surprise and anger, of dejection and fear, were partially mollified when we saw that the tables were again laid as we had first found them. Incontinently, we sat down and feasted once more.

"This will not do," said Kalu, stripping a chicken bone expertly and flinging the naked bone over his shoulder. "We are like to eat ourselves to death."

"There has to be a way," said Seg, drinking heartily.

"Aye. But which? To go left is to return to the circular room of the twelve doors. To go right is, mayhap, to return here."

"We had best try to the right. If we do return here we can go to the circular room of the twelve doors and choose again."

So we picked up our gear and set off along the way through the chamber we had not explored previously. The way led on, smoothly, until we came to a low-ceiled room, at the farther end of which was set a large door, and a smaller at its side. One, the larger, was green, and the smaller was red.

Everybody set down their burdens and waited. I felt that same prickling on me as I feel when unseen eyes smolder upon my naked back, as a great beast readies itself to spring.

I said, "The red door."

Ornol swung to face me. His pallor shone. "Red? Red—that is no color for a true Pandaheem! I choose the green!"

"Well," I said, forgetting all about niceties of address, "green is not the color of Pandahem. That is blue."

"If you seek a quarrel—"

I drew a breath. I was in for it now. Like a calsany, stubborn and onkerish, I dug my heels in.

"I go through the red door. Those who wish may go with you through the green."

Immediately, Skort chirped out: "I go with the strom."

"And I," said the sorcerer.

Kalu, quietly, said, "I will go with the Bogandur."

We all looked at Exandu. Shanli mopped his brow.

He looked at Ornol and then at me, at the large green door and the small red door. He sweated. He shook. He turned his eyes up piteously.

"Does no one then think of my poor old bones? Of my feet which are blistered to the bone? How I ache!"

Shanli whispered in his ear. He sighed.

"Very well. I mean you no offense, Strom Ornol. You, I think, understand that." And here Exandu jingled the pouch of gold he carried strapped to his waist belt. We did not miss the significance of the gesture. "But I go with Dray the Bogandur, through the red door."

Ornol's head jerked back. His nostrils pinched in.

"Very well." He swung his sword, commandingly. "Come!"

He ordered his slaves to kick the green door open. They did so. A sweet scent wafted and light shone. They all went through, two by two, warriors with swords, porters with burdens, and we heard their excited exclamations of pleasure and wonder gradually fading on the scented air.

"Perhaps . . ." stammered Exandu.

Seg turned to me, preoccupied. "Why make an issue of it now?"

"The red door just—seems right.'"

"Perhaps we ought—" Exandu started over. "They sound very jolly."

The green door slammed in our faces.

I kicked the red door open.

A dim blueish light shone at the head of a flight of stairs. Those stairs stretched wide to either side. On each tread a tall golden candelabrum upheld in clenched fists five golden candles. The flames rose, tall, sharp, flowerlike in their involuted calmness. The blue light dropped down, pervading everything that golden light did not reach. The air tanged, harsh, warningly. I stepped through and Hop the Intemperate, so close he pushed me aside a little, thrust his ten-foot pole ahead.

The pole clanged against marble. The floor of the space above the flight of stairs remained firm, unyielding.

We moved through the doorway, and paused, gazing down the stairs into a vast inchoate blueness far beneath.

The red door groaned and closed at our backs.

We were a small party; Kalu and his men, Exandu, Shanli and Hop and their people. Seg and myself. We stood looking down that breathtaking vista.

The red door groaned and closed—and the treads and risers of the stairway rotated and combined into a single long shining sheet, stretching away and away beneath—stretching into stygian blackness as all the candles were extinguished as one and the blueness vanished.

In a sliding helpless mass we shot screaming down into the blackness.

Chapter Sixteen

Red Water

Whoever crafted those steps was a master mason. There was not a fissure between tread and riser you could slide a hair through. Down that slippery slope in the utter darkness we slid, straight down, whoosh, helter-skelter, helplessly.

People slid into me, and whirled away, and the cries bounced from the roof, weirdly, echoing like bats trapped in a vault.

How long we skidded down I do not know. It could not have been much above four or five minutes; it felt like a lifetime. Without warning, smashingly, I went feet first into water. The shock knocked the breath from my lungs.

In a moment or two, with lungs aflame, I surfaced.

Flinging the hair back from my eyes and staring around I saw the darkness relieved by a somber red glow. Even as I watched and the heads began to bob up in the water alongside, the glow grew and deepened and became a blood-red drenching of fire all about.

It was borne in on me that, perhaps, just perhaps, red was not going to be the Prescot color in this pickle.

Hop the Intemperate, flailing away like a pregnant whale, surfaced, spouting.

"Help!"

I put a hand under his armpit. The armor we wore would drag us down if we did not shed it or find a landing place very quickly.

Across from me a ledge of rock showed.

"The rock!" I heaved up and bellowed. "Make for the rock."

We all started splashing. A Pachak at my side, using an economical three-handed paddle, dived away, yelling.

At his side, glimpsed in rosy silver flakings in the red light and the water a long fish shape darted.

Fangs opened wide, tiny eyes glared black and malevolent. Fins shivered silver. The great fish opened its jaws and bore in, hungrily.

Time, time! There was no time! I drew my old sailor knife and dived under. The sleek belly sped past above, and the legs of the Pachak kicked just beyond. Quickly, quickly! The sailor knife, honed to a wicked edge, sliced all along the guts of the fish. Redness poured out. I drew the knife along, and then turned, flailing my arms, shot for the surface. There was time only to see Hop scrambling up onto the ledge, and Seg hoisting Shanli up, before I'd drawn in a mighty lungful of air and so dived again.

There were more of the giant fish, wicked jaws agape, silver and red in the water, arrowing in.

Three of them, three I took.

Then I surfaced and Seg hauled me out.

Exandu was wailing and moaning—he had a slash along his left calf and he swore that his leg had been taken off for dinner.

Shanli calmed him. I was trembling. The fish had been—had been deadly, in their intent.

We huddled on the ledge and dripped water. In that ruddy light the water dropped like blood.

Pieces of fish rose to the surface and reddened the red water, and monstrous shapes fought over them, and devoured them. Hop shuddered. He stared at me as though drugged.

"You saved us all!"

"No," I said. "I took but three."

"But," he said, and pointed, "see!"

And there were many more than three fish corpses being consumed in the bloody water.

I stood up. I clutched the wall for support.

"I am going this way." I started to move. I didn't care which way we went. "Follow me."

Obediently, they stood up, shaking, and followed.

The ledge, slippery with fungoid things, broadened. We passed under an overhang and entered a series of chambers cut from the rock. Here, in the pervasive ruby light, giant and obscene carvings leered at us from every wall, from the roof, pranced at our side, seeming to move and beckon as we passed. I thought to shield Shanli from these awful sights, but she strode on, head up, supporting Exandu, not looking to right or left, but guiding his path.

Then, I thought—the people who construct these places

love to put these carvings here, and so was myself again, able to be mocking and cynical and no longer wrought up by the darkness and the ruby light and giant fish and the horror of fangs closing on naked and quivering flesh.

As we passed on I counted the people with us; we had not lost a single soul.

Forcing our way through hanging slimy growths, like seaweed, dangling at the exit to the caverns, on we went. We were attacked by reptilian things that skittered and chirped and slashed their stingers at our legs as we passed. We squashed them and moved on.

We were assailed by stenches released from corpse pits abandoned for centuries, we stopped up our nostrils and pressed on. Skeletons dangled in our path, and came to life and sought to drag us down with bony fingers. These we cut to pieces, bone by bone, limb by limb. We sundered their blasphemous forms, and went on.

In a cavern drenched in a pallid greenish light a giant dragon, a risslaca of horns and scales and tri-tails, essayed the task of slaying and eating us. Him we shot with arrows, from bows freshly strung with dry strings, and cut him with spears, and so drove him sobbing back into a rocky corner. We left him there, cowering from our spite, and did not kill him, and pressed on.

We pressed on. That was the sum of our achievement.

Our clothes were ripped and shredded and torn to pieces. Our limbs were raked by talons, and torn and bloodied. Our armor was dented. Our helmets hung lopsidedly. Many of our weapons were broken. But we pushed on, on. . . .

And, at last, a ragged scarecrow bunch, we stumbled on a stair that led upward.

"I cannot climb," declared Exandu. He sank down. "I am done for."

"Would you have Shanli carry you on her back? Would you bear that shame?"

"Shame? What shame?"

Seg stepped forward. He lifted Exandu. The man was large and well-filled, with a nose of size; Seg lifted him as he would a little child. "I will carry you up."

"Horkandur," whispered Exandu. "Horkandur."

So, up the stairs we went, and we went carefully, for we had had our bellyful of tricks and traps.

At the top a small red door stood before us. I did not kick it in with casual violence. We looked all about, and we prodded with our poles. We pushed the door with a pole from a safe distance. And we were quiet and we listened.

The door eased open.

Red light shafted out.

Kalu, at my side, took a breath. "We have been through much, Bogandur. But there is worse to come."

"In that case," I said, and I own to that old Prescot madness upon me, "we will front it now!"

And I bashed the door open and leaped through.

I did not die. I am here to prove that.

I would have done so if Seg, ready with arrow notched and drawn, had not loosed with deadly aim.

Yet the fellow who would have had me was only a normal human being, a malko, a ferocious gorilla-faced chap with massive muscles, of a stocky, dour, indrawn disposition. He dropped on me from above the door, and his curved sword slashed for my throat.

Seg's shaft took him clear through his back, punched on through lungs and chest and shattered out in a splattering gush of blood. I slashed sideways as I rolled clear.

The room was wide, bright with lanterns, and a dozen more of the gorilla-faced malkos ran up, weapons glittering.

These were only men, ferocious, and armed; they were nothing compared with the terrors through which we had passed. Seg stepped up, shooting like a fountain of shafts, and Hop surged alongside me, with Kalu on the other side, and his Pachaks with him. The fight was brief and exceedingly ferocious. At its conclusion the malkos lay dead, and, still we had not lost a warrior.

Sweat and blood bedabbled us. We glared at the high-domed chamber under the lights.

Along one side a row of cages stood, black-barred and empty. A few tables and benches, strewn with discarded scraps of food and warrior trappings, huddled in one corner. Seven doors opened at the far end. Nearer at hand, a door stood in an angle. The air held a cloying, stale smell.

"I must have a drink," cried Exandu. He lay where Seg had dropped him. Shanli cooed over him. Kalu stepped out into the hall, his warriors with him, and they carried out a swift but thorough search. I crossed to the door in the angle.

"Take care, Bogandur," called Seg.

He stood at my back, arrow to string, half drawn, ready.

I did not say, as it crossed my mind to do, "With you at

my back, Seg, I have no need for care." Cautiously, I pushed open the door with my sword.

A corridor lay exposed. The light was not as bright. A fresh rotting smell gusted out. Four doors broke the left-hand wall, and one to the right lay recessed, with a red lamp above the arch. I stepped forward.

Stepping with exquisite care, testing every footfall, I inched along to look into the barred opening of the first door. The cell lay empty, straw-strewn and stinking.

The second cell contained a skeleton, cruelly chained to the wall.

The third cell held a woman.

She stared up as I looked in. She held herself with such commanding power, clad in rags, her hair stringy and tangled, that my heart leaped. She stared with a bright and hostile arrogance upon me as I peered in through the bars.

The cell door was barred from the outside. I lifted the bar, in a gesture at once matching her arrogance, and pitiful in my instinctive reaction. I lifted the bar and threw it aside.

A sliding screech sounded in my ears.

Instantly I hurled myself headlong, fingers scrabbling for the edge of the pit the trapdoor beneath my feet opened.

Only a catlike swiftness saved me. I caught the edge and hung. Dangling, I hung there as the harsh croaking voices of malkos sounded, gobbling in glee. They broke from the recessed door with the red light above it. They swarmed across the corridor, their weapons lifted, their gorilla faces alive with sadistic glee at my plight and their solution to my problem.

Suspended over a gulf which at its floor held a bed of spikes, I did not doubt, if nothing worse, I saw the onrush of the guards. There were six of them. They wielded spears and axes. They rushed.

My muscles cracked as I sought to lever myself up.

Seg's bow loosed. With blurring speed he loosed again. Two of the malkos pitched forward, skewered. Then Seg, with a bellow of pure rage, hurled himself forward. His sword flamed. I got an elbow up, then the other, chinned myself over the lip and rolled. Seg's blade clashed violently with the axe of the first malko, twirled and thrust. A spear slashed down Seg's side and he reeled away, and came back, raging. I was up on a knee. The next malko sought to smash Seg's brains out, and was punctured for his pains. The others closed in, and for a moment Seg was slashing and hacking, leaping and ducking, a magnificent fighting warrior, battling for his life and the life of his comrade.

Then I got myself—tardily, tardily!—into action and dinted the last of them. He fell full length with a clash of armor.

Seg shooshed a great breath, and wiped a bloody hand across his face. His sword dripped.

"Hai, Jikai!" cried the woman, walking from her cell. "I give you the High Jikai!"

"My lady!" said Seg.

"Aye," I said, speaking with a rush. "And I give you the High Jikai, too, Seg."

We stood for a moment, there in that blood-soaked corridor in a place of horrors, and took our breath. Then Seg said, "Llahal, my lady. I am Seg. And this is Dray."

She managed a smile. She did not look at the mangled corpses. "You are welcome. You have come with a strong party of warriors to rescue the king and queen?"

"Well, no, my lady," said Seg.

"But you must have! Why else would you venture into the Coup Blag, this vile place in the Snarly Hills?"

I said, "There is gold, my lady, and treasure."

She looked stunned. Then, "You have not seen the king, the queen? Or any of—their people?"

"Only a poor devil of a Pachak, who died."

We must have looked like very devils, ourselves, Seg and me. We were battle-stained, blood-splashed, grimed and sweaty. Our swords reeked. We were big, muscle-bulging fellows with hardy looks and uncommon quick ways. She sucked in her breath.

Seg said, "My lady. Our swords are at your command."

"Yes, yes, jikais. But—those poor people—I came here with the queen to look for the king. We did not find him. We found horror and death. And the bandits were too frightened—"

"Yes," I said. "Do not fret over them now."

Seg began to wipe his sword on the tunic of a slain malko. I did the same. We were careful to wipe our hands and the hilts of our sword, scrupulous in cleansing them.

The woman said, "Lahal, you must forgive me." She swayed. "My name is Milsi and I serve Queen Mab. And you are drikingers, also."

"Lahal, Milsi," said Seg. "No. No, we are not bandits."

"But—"

And then Exandu tottered along, staring at the corpses and mopping his brow.

"Careful of that great hole in the floor," said Seg.

"What—" He saw Milsi. "A woman, Seg the Horkandur?"

"Aye," said Seg. "The lady Milsi."

She had said she served Queen Mab and it was quite clear from her demeanor and carriage that she was no serving wench. She looked with some curiosity upon Exandu, and, in truth, he looked like us, a right bundle of rags and blood.

She addressed Seg, and he instantly attended to her, bending only a little, his face intent.

"The next cell. Would you look, please?"

"The bar—" I warned.

"Aye."

Seg looked in and I peered over his shoulder. A corpse of a woman, half-naked, with long dark hair astrew, lay collapsed against the wall. Seg turned at once.

The woman sighed at his face.

"So she is dead, then—a friend—oh, this hideous place!"

And Seg put his arms about the lady Milsi, and comforted her.

Kalu and his people came in then to report that nothing stirred in the chamber. We had seven doors from which to make a choice. Which would it be?

"My lady," said Seg, and I marveled at the gentleness of his voice in these horrific surroundings. "You have knowledge of this place? This maze of the Coup Blag?"

She pulled back a little from him and looked up, and the tears stood in her eyes. "No. No, I do not know—I know only that we must find the king—and the queen—and leave with our lives—if we can."

"We must do more than that," put in Kalu, with his usual cheerfulness. He appeared undaunted by the terrors through which we had gone. "I, for one, do not intend to leave without my fair share of treasure."

"But—your life—?"

"I have risked it many times, my lady. It is a habit."

About to turn away and make a start on the next door, I swung back as Seg spoke. He spoke to the lady Milsi.

"Lady. Your life will be mine—while I live no harm shall come to you if I can prevent it. That I swear."

Abruptly, like lightning striking through thunderclouds, she smiled. She was splendid in that moment. "You will be my jikai, Seg the Horkandur?"

"If you wish it, lady."

They stood, looking one at the other, and I knew they did not see and were not aware of anyone else.

Softly, she said, "I wish it."

Chapter Seventeen

Milsi

We stood before the seven doors and Exandu said, "You choose red again, Bogandur? After the travails we suffered because of that red door at the head of the staircase?" He cocked his head at me, his nose red as the door before which we stood. "Blue or green are the colors of Pandahem."

"As they are of Hamal, master Exandu."

"That I grant you. But red—I do not think my aching bones, my head, my feet, my heart or liver will stand any further torments."

"There will be more, Exandu," said Kalu. "Never fear."

The lady Milsi stood close by Seg. She said. "He is mightily cheerful." She turned to Kalu. "Why is that, Pachak?"

"My lady?" Kalu Na-Fre looked perplexed. "Why should one be concerned over death? Papachak has all mortals in his hands. There is treasure here, and my bonny fellows will bring it out."

"Or die in the attempt?"

"If that is willed." Kalu gestured at the doors. "I have followed pantor Dray and with him Exandu and pantor Seg. I do not think I shall change now. They have brought me luck."

"Luck!" burst out Exandu. Shanli soothed him, and Hop the Intemperate let out a gusty kind of laughing groan.

"Certainly. I have not lost a single one of my fine fellows since we left that Strom Ornol."

The lady Milsi put a hand to her face. Seg instantly put his arm about her waist to support her. She was a splendid woman, her body, although grimed with dirt, glowing through the rents in her clothes, full and firm and voluptuous. She was of an age with Seg, I judged, probably a few seasons younger, given that Seg had bathed in the River of Baptism in far Aphrasöe, and therefore one must judge his age not by chronology but by his appearance when he bathed in that magical stream.

"Very well, then," spoke out Exandu, and he drew himself up. "Red it is." Then he said, "It will bring back the memories."

Using the skills we had acquired to stay living people in this place, this abode of horrors called the Coup Blag, we pushed the door open. Only a stone-walled corridor showed before us, ten feet high and broad, stretching some fifty feet to the corner, unbroken by doors. We entered and, prodding and watching, went on.

We found a few traps, things of swinging flagstones in the floor, and spyholes with crossbow bolts fixed to loose at anyone passing, and a metal mirror fixed at forty-five degrees so that what we thought was the end of the tunnel was a pit filled with acid. These traps we negotiated, and pressed on. The sound of voices, and singing, and the clink of bottles and glasses reached us from around the next bend.

"Anyone for the Cabaret?" said Seg, and he laughed.

The lady Milsi walked now with her arm about his waist, and he assisted her along with great solicitude.

I stuck my head around the corner.

The chamber was large, filled with light. There were tables laid for a feast. They were there, sprawled out, eating and drinking and singing. Chests stood ranked and broken open and a profusion of treasures had been pulled out and lay scattered on the marble flooring. The smells of food and wine struck us shrewdly.

Strom Ornol looked up. His pallid face showed a flush along the cheekbones and he waved a golden goblet high.

"So there you are! We thought you were all dead."

We walked forward.

Fregeff and Rik Razortooth were drinking, one a good rosé and the other a silver dish of blood. I could not see Skort the Clawsang.

"Skort?" said Ornol. "Oh, he disappeared some time ago. We had a wonderful time in a valley choked with fruit trees and filled with flowers. Then we came in here and have been feasting ever since. We move on soon. You are only just in time." He saw the lady Milsi.

"Oh?"

The pappattu was made. Milsi was seated next to the lady Ilsa, and we men heard words concerning fresh clothes.

"It is rest we need!" declared Seg hotly.

"Well, that is your fault for not following me. We have had a splendid time, and we think we know the way out."

"Bogandur!" cried Exandu, collapsing into a chair. "What have you done to me!"

"We will be happy to go with you, Strom Ornol," I said. "After we have eaten and taken our rest."

Fregeff ostentatiously reached for a fresh dish of blood.

Kalu said, "Where is the way out?" He stared at the treasures scattered about. "There is some treasure here. But we have not had a hard time yet, and the end of this is not yet in sight."

"Not had a hard time!" exclaimed Shanli. "Look at my poor master! Shame on you, master Kalu!"

And the Pachak laughed, and swirled his tail hand, and went off with his people to eat and drink.

"The way out lies the way we entered," said Ornol.

"Perhaps," said Kalu, and took up a golden goblet and drank deeply.

Ornol transferred his attention to Milsi, and her story was soon told. Ornol sneered. "Serving a king or queen is a poor man's game. There is no real reward in that."

Seg stiffened. "At least, when they kick out ne'er-do-wells, they usually have their reasons."

There would have been a fight, there and then, if we others had not intervened. Ornol didn't know how lucky he was.

Sucking at a honeyed wine, Exandu moaned as Shanli wiped his brow. "If only we'd gone with Ornol through the green door, think of the misery and terror we would have been spared!"

"Yes," I said. "Perhaps I did not choose wisely—save in one thing."

"Aye," said Seg, with a snap in his voice. "Had we gone through the green door, we would never have—"

Milsi laid her hand on his arm. He turned, at once, looking at her. She smiled. "I will go with the lady Ilsa and make myself presentable. I have much to thank you and Dray the Bogandur for, Seg the Horkandur, jikai."

Seg rolled his shoulders most uncomfortably under that.

"My lady . . ." was all he could find to say.

"Anyway," Kalu was saying between mouthfuls to Hop, "where I come from the hellhounds breathe fire. They'll crisp you up like a vosk rasher."

"That is sorcery, Kalu, I daresay."

"Ask Fregeff."

I walked along and took up a piece of meat and ate, what it was I've no idea, and regarded Ornol from the corner of my eye. If the idiot insisted on rushing off at once, I did not think the party with me was in fit state to follow. And, the lady Ilsa provided a pretty problem, too. . . .

Kalu laughed, and so drew my attention. "Very well, Hop the Intemperate. When we all get out of here, I'll make an assignation with you at The Sign of the Jolly Puddler in Mahendrasmot. Is it a bargain?"

"If we get out—"

"You stick with me and my fine fellows. No fear of that."

Some of the warriors were singing "My Love is like a Moon Bloom." A rival party at the other table struck up with "The Two-Tailed Kataki," which made Seg glance quickly down the chamber to where the ladies were fussing over chests of gorgeous raiment.

"She's a grown-up girl," I said to Seg.

He did not flush; but he looked decidedly off key.

"You—like her, Dray?"

"Yes."

"Since I lost Thelda, I've not really bothered to look at another woman. But I'm over Thelda now. She is a part of the past. I shan't forget her; but—"

"Milsi is a splendid woman, Seg. By Vox! She's been through a few horrors down here. Yet she's—well, she's—"

"Aye!"

"All the same. She has a past, too."

"I know. I think she is in much the same case as I am."

I put a hand on Seg's shoulder. This was an unusual and gratuitous gesture between us; but I was deeply moved. He smiled that smile of his, and his fey blue eyes challenged me. "All right, my old dom. I do not forget you owe me a faceful of dungy straw."

"Two!" I said. "Two, by Zair!"

And we both recalled that fraught day in The Eye of the World when the Sorzarts raided the farm and we first met.

The merriment thundered on. These people were reacting to moments of horror, snatching a few balancing moments of boisterous pleasure before plunging once more into the terrors of the Coup Blag. We set about filling our bellies and of finding fresh clothing and weaponry.

Needless to say, Seg and I found some scarlet cloth, and so

fashioned ourselves breechclouts in the color that—well, that might this time just have proved itself once again.

Among the merrymakers the absence of decomposing corpse-faces was marked. We asked questions, and learned that Skort and his people, with some of the porters, had been bringing up the rear guard when a stone block had fallen across the corridor. The delayed-action trap had squashed only two poor fellows, a Rapa and a Moltingur; but it had isolated Skort from the rest.

"This is a maze," declared Fregeff. "Doubtless we will come upon them again."

"I sincerely hope so," I said, munching on a hunk of roast vosk leg. "The Clawsangs are bonny fighters."

The pressure Exandu could bring to bear on Ornol must now be lessened, at least in the young dandy's eyes, by reason of the treasure here. He could be free of what he owed. All the same, Exandu managed to persuade the strom to wait until we were in better shape to march with him.

At last, fully kitted out and feeling rested, we took up our bundles of loot and started out.

Up ahead along a corridor, and nastily soon after we started, we heard Ornol's strident voice.

"By the Furnace Fires of Inshurfraz!" he screamed. "Is there no way out of this maze?"

We were back in the room of the feast from which we had started.

"We try another door, pantor," said Kalu, equably.

So we did. This time we followed on into corridors we had not penetrated before. The little mark of the heart had long since petered out. Whoever had made it had not ventured these halls and passages of dread.

When we came across levers and buttons and tripwires we left them severely alone. We halted, as our way was impeded by a simple tilting flagstone trap. A prod from a pole dipped the near edge down without effort. It swung lazily back into place. The stone was too wide to clear with a jump. To balance two men would be exceptionally tricky.

Standing in a niche cut from the rock stood the armored skeleton of a Chulik. He looked ferocious, pared to the bone. If he was touched, warned Fregeff, who could guess the magic there, he would probably come to life and we'd have an unwanted fight on our hands with a fearsome representative of the Kaotim, the Undead, who are well known on Kregen.

Kalu stepped forward. "I am not so sure," said the Pachak. "Pantor Dray, would you stand ready to cut his legs away from under him? And, Pantor Seg—?"

We, with others, poised our weapons ready to slash the skeleton to pieces the instant it moved.

Kalu reached out with his sword and, delicately, pushed the skeleton's skull. The jawbone clicked up into place.

Nothing else happened.

"There!" cried Kalu, and his tail hand pointed at the swinging stone trap. "Try it now!"

We did. The flagstone held firmly for us all to cross.

We crossed that trap in safety, but others caught us and men died. I misliked this greatly, but after another blazing row with Ornol over directions, we all went along a smoothly paved and open passageway and I trailed on after.

Seg said, "Should we cut off on our own?"

"Safety in numbers. Anyway—apart from Milsi—he was right about the large green and small red doors."

Around about then the passageway opened into a chamber robed in yellow silk, with an ebon throne surrounded by skulls and with tall candles burning. Kalu looked around and yawned.

When a horned and hoofed demon, of the horrific Kregan variety, appeared from nowhere on that ebon throne, Kalu took a little more interest in the proceedings.

Being of Kregen, the demon was hooved of rear feet, clawed of third feet, tentacled of second feet and bore human hands on his forearms. His horns emitted sparks of light. His tongue licked out like a rattlesnake. Everyone screamed and crowded for the door by which we had entered—everyone save Fregeff, the Fristle sorcerer.

He lifted his bronzen flail and shook it and the demon struck with a twinned bolt of fire from his eyes and poor Fregeff went thump head over heels into the corner.

The pandemonium at the door sorted itself out as the crazed mob fled. More than one wretch fell and was trampled.

Fregeff crawled painfully to his feet. His eyes streamed blood. But he lifted the flail, and shook it.

The twin blue bolts of fire hurled him flat again.

Seg loosed a shaft. It caromed off the demon, who took no notice.

I said, "You'd best take the lady Milsi out, Seg."

"And leave you?"

"Oh, I'll run with the best of you. But—Fregeff—"

"He has met his match."

"I am not so sure—look!"

For the Fristle gathered himself together. His arm lifted. He released the bronzen chain attached to the collar about the reptile's neck. The volschrin on his shoulder spread his wings. Rik Razortooth swooped up in a sudden gusting of membranous wings.

As Fregeff shook his flail for the third time, the demon uttered a screech of pure rage. The twin blue bolts of devil fire slashed from his eyes, burned across the chamber. The sorcerer flopped over, his lozenged robes flapping. He twitched an arm. Again the bolts of fire flew from the demon's lambent eyes. But this time they struck for the volschrin. Rik swerved in midair, dived and weaved and the hissing blue bolts of lethal fire missed. Fregeff shook his flail weakly.

Rik dodged the last outpouring of malevolent energy and then—and then! The reptile simply flew straight at the demon's face. Sharp fangs slashed. First one eye and then the other shredded. They did not bleed. They exploded into blue flame and Rik somersaulted away, wing over wing, to gain his balance in the air and so volplane easily to Fregeff's shoulder.

The Fristle reached up his left hand and caressed the little winged reptile.

The demon stood up. Now blood, blue, smoking blood, poured down his cheeks from his ruined eyes. He shrieked. He tried to fly away with jagged wings and crashed into the throne and darts of glittering steel sliced from the sides of the throne and impaled him. The defense of the throne slew its occupant.

The demon collapsed like a slashed wine sack.

The seven hoops of steel, razor-sharp, met through his gross body.

Fregeff stood up.

Seg, Milsi, and I ran to him.

"San! San—you are unharmed?"

"As well as can be expected." And the Fristle laughed.

The laugh bordered on hysteria; but Rik flapped his wings and Fregeff was instantly himself. His face with its fierce whiskers looked drawn. His hands shook.

"The little volschrin," said Seg, "he is a marvel."

Because wizards, even good wizards, are not all sweetness

and light, it was perfectly natural for Fregeff to say, "Yes. Beware lest he take your eyes."

We heard the hiss of indrawn breath at our backs, and, instantly, Seg and I whirled, swords snouting. Kalu stood there, his own weapons raised. His Pachak face, hard, dedicated, revealed more emotion than any we had so far seen him express.

"Demons!" he said. Had the thought not been incongruous, I would have thought he spoke with joy. "Now that is more like an adventure!"

His own people had remained with him; now they began to retire through the doorway. Fregeff shook himself, refastened the bronze linked chain to Rik's collar, and, with the reptile flappingly settling back onto his shoulder, nodded to us and went out. Seg took Milsi's arm.

"Time to go—"

"Yes. A moment, Seg. Those guards, those malkos, down in the cells. They were—different—from the rest of this infernal maze." I faced the lady Milsi. "Were they the bandits, do you know, my lady?"

"I—I do not know. My party was set on and my people were killed, or ran. I was taken up, prisoner, and conducted to that awful place."

"So you cannot know anything of the maze. No, I see that. Still, I wonder why they imprisoned you—"

"I serve the queen—"

"No good will come of this now, Dray! Come on, my old dom. Let's get out of this place and see about looking for the way out. There has to be one, somewhere."

"You are right. Lead on."

I turned toward the doorway and followed Seg and Milsi as they left. A movement caught at the corner of my left eye, and I looked that way, ready for a sudden treacherous onslaught.

One of the tall yellow silk drapes hanging against the wall rippled its sinuous length. I waited for a moment, watchfully. A small brown and red scorpion waddled out from under the drape. He stopped, looked about, waving his tail over his head. Then, as my indrawn breath hissed, he turned around and strutted delicately back, the stinger like a mocking finger upraised. He vanished under the yellow silk.

I felt the blood go thump around my body. A sliding, grating screech of stone on stone sounded in the chamber. I faced the door again. A slab of stone slid down between the door jambs. It hit the floor with a solid thud.

My sword rang uselessly against the stone.

I was alone in the chamber, trapped behind solid rock.

A sound whispered at my back. I whirled. The seven hoops of razor-sharp steel slid back into the ebon throne. They sucked themselves from the demon's body with a bright glitter, unstained by blood, blue or red. The streaks of blood upon the demon's cheeks, smoking, ran upward. They drew themselves up and entered the ruined sockets of his eyes. And when all the blood had been returned, the eyes grew back again, blazing devilish eyes of fearful hate.

The demon hissed. He came to life and roared, and those evil eyes flamed with sorcerous power from another world.

Alone, trapped, I stared with fearful fascination upon the ghastly form of the demon as he prepared to blast me where I stood.

Chapter Eighteen

Pitched into the Depths

I, Dray Prescot, Lord of Strombor and Krozair of Zy, felt all the blood in my body congeal. My heart thudded with pain. I trembled. The eyes of the demon mesmerized me. Sparks flew from those orbs, gigantic orbs, swelling and bloating with power. In the next heartbeat—if my heart could ever beat again—supernal bolts of fire would lash from those eyes and burn me to a crisp.

There was just one chance, just the one, and the little brown and red scorpion was my only hope.

Headlong, I dived for the yellow silk curtain from which the scorpion had so delicately waddled.

No time to lift the drape. No time to do anything but hurl myself full at the wall.

My shoulder hit the yellow silk. It bulged inward. For a frightful moment I thought I had thrown myself against solid rock—for I went smashing into a hard surface. Then—and even as I burst in a shower of plaster through the false wall—a scorching fire flamed past my back.

The demon had hurled his bolts of lambent fire and the yellow silk burst into flame. Amid a shower of broken plaster and splintered lathes, I tumbled head over heels out of the demon's lair and into a chute down which I slid end over end, spinning around like a Catherine Wheel, arms and legs splaying like a drunken crab.

Lurid flames played above me as the silk wisped and more bolts of fire lashed at the opening I had made.

I hit something soft and furry and warm. Yellow torchlight blazed in my eyes. I felt the warm furry object move and lurch. In the next instant I was gripping on for dear life as a monstrous beast went screeching and trumpeting away along a corridor. Horns lifting before me, tail lashing to my rear, a gross body waddling from side to side beneath me, trapped

144

on the back of an immense and savage beast, I went shooting away along the passage under the streaming light of the torches.

By Zair! This was a nightmare come true! I gripped on and shook my head and swallowed and so looked about to see what I could do—if anything.

What manner of beast it was that I bestrode in so strange a fashion I could not tell. I clung on and got my breath, and saw the roof of the tunnel lowering and narrowing ahead.

In only moments at the speed we were going the beast would be into the lower portion of the tunnel and I'd be scraped off as a dog scrapes off a flea against a rough tree trunk.

I swiveled around. The stone floor whistled past. I took a breath, lay flat and then rolled off aft. A tail lashed at me and winded me, and I hit the floor and bounced like a rubber ball. I tumbled hard, head over heels, and lay for a moment, flat, staring at the disappearing beast. I could see flailing tail and galloping clawed feet, and a mass of shaggy hair, and that was all. The monstrous beast dived into the narrow tunnel and vanished around a corner.

I sat up. The tunnel stopped going around, and settled for up being up and down being down. I felt myself and decided that if I had any broken bones they wouldn't stop me from marching on and out of this Coup Blag nightmare.

And then I realized just where I was.

How often I have said that I like to be off adventuring alone! How often I have boasted emptily that to be off by myself is the height of joy! Well, right now I wished I was still with my companions. This maze of monsters and demons, of savage beasts and cunning traps, was no place to be alone.

No, by Zair!

Still, I had to go on. Quite apart from the mystery of Spikatur Hunting Sword, and the onrushing menace of the Shanks and their tremendous invasion fleet, there was the question of my life. That, I felt, was something I ought to ponder on.

As I picked myself up and settled my gear straight, I found myself wondering if, perhaps, that scorpion was another sign from the Star Lords. Could that incident have been a simple coincidence? It did not seem likely.

In the flaring yellow light of the torches becketed along the walls I looked about carefully. The tunnel contained jagged openings on my right, as though the rock had been broken open. Light splashed inside. Of course, I said to myself with little satisfaction, of course—stupid to imagine the Star Lords would actually help me, even recognize me, despite what had happened to my recent astonishment. Anyway—if that damned scorpion hadn't waddled out so insolently from the silk drape, I would not have hesitated and would have left the demon's lair.

The scorpion had not just saved me, he'd damned well got me trapped in the first place.

Exploring the jagged openings and the maze of tunnels beyond was a chancy business. The torches burned with their yellow light, and I ran constantly across nasties, ferocious animals and beast-men, fanged and clawed, dripping horrors of nightmare. Now, meaningfully, I wielded the superb Krozair longsword and I did not hesitate. The moment any malign creatures confronted me, it was a headlong blattering attack that swept them away in lethal bites of the magnificent Krozair brand.

"By the Black Chunkrah," I said, sweeping my hair back, staring in foul temper at the latest dismembered corpse of a hairy horror, "I can't spend all my life shilly-shallying about down here!"

But that seemed all too likely a prospect as I went stumbling on. In a section of tunnel from which the roof had fallen, to admit a green leprous light like a radiant leaching stripping away flesh from bone, I ran across some poor devil who had not jumped fast enough.

Off to the side and inclined down from a higher level ran a quadruple-chute. The slide was of a greenish metal, well-oiled, sharp-angled. On the floor at my feet rested a massive object like a bobbin with four sections, one to fit each part of the chute. The bobbin was man-high in diameter. Under it blood had congealed. A pair of legs stuck out, the sandals worn and with a leather strap broken and tied up over the big toe of the left foot. Also a hand stuck out here, grasping a ten-foot pole.

The fellow's fingers had to be broken to release the pole. He wore no rings.

I pondered.

The ten-foot pole had failed him. It seemed to me that I was on a low level of the Coup Blag, perhaps at the basement level. Up higher—and, by Krun! I was going up higher!—the traps would be clustered thickly to precipitate unfortunates back down here. I took the ten-foot pole and scabbarded the longsword.

In only a few hundred yards I came across stone steps leading up.

I stopped.

Now stairs are the very devil for traps.

You can put your foot down and instead of treading on solid stone, you break through painted parchment and get caught in a bear trap. You can trigger a pressure plate, and the step at your back will gape open and something exceedingly hard and sharp will come flying out and knock you sideways to breakfast time. You can be caught as we had already been caught, in a stairway that snaps shut into a slippery slope. Stairs can be counter-balanced and geared to a pack of half-starved krahniks who treadmill away like crazy, so that you run and run and the stairway whistles back so that you do not move forward an inch.

And, inevitably, there are the stairways that deluge foul-smelling gunk on you from on high when you reach a certain tread or acid that eats you or nauseating gas that chokes you. As I say, beware of lightly tripping up and down stairs. . . .

Prodding carefully, up I went.

This little beauty was fixed to trigger crossbow bolts through holes in the risers. The bolts were arranged to make diced meat of anyone foolish enough to trigger the bows. The ten-foot pole worked and the bolts hissed over my head. I own I stopped, then, and swallowed. Still, up I had to go. . . .

The corridor at the top was almost like coming home after the jagged uncertainties of the caverns beneath.

The first room contained a single table, spread with fine linen, set out with a sumptuous meal—for one.

Not having a handy slave to taste the meal, and being starving hungry, I set to. If precedent was to be followed, I should be all right. Who or whatever was monitoring proceedings here was well aware of my predicament. No doubt methods of observations were fixed everywhere. This argued that the powers of a great wizard were at work. The signomants by which Wizards of Loh are able to see events at vast distances must be here, somewhere, but I could not discover them.

The little signomant like a bronze brooch with nine differently colored gems given me by my comrade Wizard of Loh, Khe-Hi-Bjanching, had been long since lost. Probably my friends were able to investigate the bottom of a river, or the depths of a swamp. I tramped on, wiping my mouth, and twirled the ten-foot pole in readiness for the next set of alarums and excursions.

Worries over Seg had to be pushed aside. He was with the main party and they had Kalu and the sorcerer Fregeff, and they should manage to keep themselves sane and alive. Moving along and prodding and keeping a watchful eye on everything, I considered the consequences of the eruption into our lives of the lady Milsi. Of course, Seg was the finest gentleman you could ever hope to meet, in the best sense, and his natural concern for Milsi was understandable. All the same, she had warmed to him. I'd seen that. She had been incarcerated, in rags, ill-used, expecting a hideous fate, and a hero had appeared and vanquished her enemies and brought her out of her imprisonment. Yes, there had been a spark in Milsi's eyes when she looked on Seg Segutorio.

Praise be to Zair!

If Seg was really interested in Milsi, then I prayed that her reciprocal interest was not merely engendered by the circumstances and a full heart of relief at her rescue, but would continue. That, only the fates and the future could tell.

Just about then the ten-foot pole came in handy in an unexpected way.

I'd negotiated a silly forty-five-degree metal mirror across the corridor and so had not gone thumping on. Ahead of me the corridor narrowed to something between five and ten feet wide. At its far end, well-lighted, the end wall was covered in two-foot-long spikes. They were clumped together like the spines of a bristle ball. I prodded the floor.

The stone appeared solid. But why stud a vertical end of a corridor with spikes, if they were not to pierce human flesh? And, if that was their function, how was I to be propelled onto them, or they to be hurled at me?

The answer came as the whole corridor tilted down.

Had the trap worked—well, had it worked you would not be listening to my narrative—I'd have gone head over heels down the vertical corridor as it swiveled into a pit, and so spread myself against the spikes, with piercing results.

The ten-foot-pole switched up like a quarterstaff and the ends cracked against the lip of the pit.

I dangled from the pole, balanced, as it held across the mouth of stone. If one end slipped . . . If I shifted my grips clumsily . . . I swung about like a pendulum over the spike-shafted pit and started to work hand over hand to the side. With a heave and a grunt I hauled myself out and reclaimed my faithful old ten-foot-pole. By Krun! The trap had been a dilly, a whole corridor suddenly plummeting down to form a deep shaft—and the spikes at the end were sharp enough and close enough to make diced Dray Prescot a reality.

Still, it had not been clever enough. The designer should have disguised the spikes. They had alerted a warning. And, I promised myself, when I met the designer of this maze, if I did, I'd let him investigate a few spikes of my own.

Then the ill-begotten child of a muck farm and a cesspool almost had me.

The trap was the same—a simple-seeming corridor that abruptly pitched down into a deadly shaft. Except that it was different. The shaft gaped before me in the center of a room, with dangling stink-vines and rotting corpses to insure I walked along where I was expected to walk.

And the shaft was ten feet wide.

As I pitched forward, the dangling screen of creepers ahead of me whisked aside to reveal the serried mass of spikes onto which I was supposed to fall.

The good old ten-foot pole caught at both ends on the sides of the shaft and stuck. It jammed across. And I dangled from the middle.

The pole was not exactly diametrically positioned across the pit. The famous ten-foot pole was by a hand's breadth longer than ten feet!

After that it was a hand-over-hand swing to reach the sheer wall. Then a muscle-jerk and a chin-up and then a balancing act on the pole. I stood up on it, pressed against the wall, and hooked my fingers over the lip above me. Hauling myself out and twisting on my stomach at the top, I looked down. I did not wish to leave the jammed pole where it was.

One end was that life-saving fraction higher than the other. I reached down, and then, with a curse at my own stupidity, took off my belt and dangled that down to catch the end of the pole and that was not long enough, either. So I joined up enough of my belts and straps and swung the end down and caught it as it looped, and slid a buckle on, and pulled it all tight.

The faithful pole came up like a gaffed salmon.

An itchy scrabbling sound at my back made me roll over without even looking for the source of the noise. I rolled and came up on a knee and the longsword pointed—and a little schrafter, an animal that sharpens his teeth on the bones of skeletons in dungeons, scuttled away, scared out of his wits.

My breath gusted out in a whoosh.

Fitting my gear together did not take long, and all the time I kept looking under and between the hanging stench vines and the grotesque half-decomposed corpse-shapes. Out there the darkness closed in. And, pair by pair, in fours and eights and scores, lambent yellow eyes gathered. When I fastened the last buckle and was ready, hundreds of pairs of eyes gleamed on me from the darkness.

Flinging a torch snatched from a corpse's withered fingers, I backed off. Careful, careful! The room offered no way forward, so I retraced my steps, turning every now and then to hurl a torch back into the host of eyes which followed in the darkness. The trouble was, flinging torches made the darkness at my back more intense. How long this went on I do not know; I know I felt more tired than a galley slave after a stern chase in a calm.

The traps I encountered when I branched off from the path I had already traversed were of the diabolical and cunning kind. Somehow I survived them, losing bits of skin, and the drexer—which annoyed me—and sundry portions of my gear. By the time I staggered into a room lit by a crystal fire roof, I had shaken off that pack of following eyes, and had also been reduced to a scarlet breechclout, a rapier—the main gauche had been carried off in the throat of a batlike creature that in swooping from the darkness had impaled itself—and the Krozair longsword. I was barefoot. Well, that is normal for a fellow who has been a powder monkey in Nelson's Navy. I staggered into this room to see three walls lined by bronze statues of armored men, apim, diff, all kinds, and the small table laid with a meal. I just flopped down on the chair and stared at the food, summoning my energies to eat and drink.

When I began to eat, if all the statues in the chamber had come to life and rushed upon me, I'd have finished gnawing on the vosk bone and fought the pack of 'em one-handed.

I drank hugely—a light Tardalvoh—and looked around the walls. And then I noticed that dust lay thickly upon the floor.

This was something new in the Coup Blag.

The wall containing the doorway through which I had entered held six other doors, all closed. They were all blue. I sighed. "By Makki-Grodno's disgusting diseased liver and lights! Is there no end to this infernal maze?"

A voice from the air said, "Blue instead of red, will serve me, will serve you, will serve destiny."

No use in looking around. The voice could be coming from anywhere. I shouted, "I'm not interested in serving destiny! I've been doing that ever since I came to Kregen! I just want to get out and go home!"

And then I checked myself. No. No, that was not true. Well, of course it was true—of course I wanted to go home to Delia. But I had to do something drastic about this confounded conspiracy of Spikatur Hunting Sword, if I killed myself doing it. I stood up, hand on sword hilt.

"Blue, you say, you misshapen Opaz-forsaken lump of—"

"If you trust me."

There was no denying the mockery. I drew a breath, stared at the doors—and, lo! All save one turned red.

I stumped across the floor, reaching for the ten-foot pole and remembering it had splintered to pieces down some damned alley. I hefted the Krozair longsword. I have used that superb brand to do all kinds of tasks on Kregen; now it would tap tap tap at the floor and walls as I went along as though I were a blind man. Which, in this place of horrors, I was.

The blue door opened before I reached it.

Blue light spilled.

Sword ready, I stormed through—and was instantly set on by a dozen of the malko guards, raging, weapons bright, gorilla fangs clashing for my throat, swords raking for my guts.

Chapter Nineteen

The Game Is Named

The very violence of their onslaught worked in my favor.

The leaders jostled one another to get at me, the blood lust bright and ugly on their lowering gorillalike faces.

Hard, packed with muscle, malkos, fierce and not to be trifled with. Big, husky fellows, with their tiny black eyes overhung with massive brow ridges, and black fissured lips, dented in by the jut of yellow fangs, glowing with a sullen passion to kill.

They wore studded leather armor, very spiky as to shoulder and elbow, bulging over ribcages, adorned with scaled belts and gilt buckles. Their weapons were spears and shields, swords and daggers, and they gobbled in their passion to slay.

I daresay they had never met a man armed with a Krozair longsword before. I venture to suggest they had never tangled with a Krozair Brother before. Well, few folk outside the inner sea of Kregen, the Eye of the World, have had that dubious pleasure. I did not waste time. The Krozair brand flamed.

When it was done, two, at least, ran screaming. They did not run with all their bodily parts intact or functioning; but they were able to run away. Their companions lay scattered about the chamber. And forgive me, I mean scattered.

By Zair! The things a man does when he is frustrated!

The malko guards, grim with their gorilla faces and their metal-studded leather armor, had been posted to watch over a series of cages. These iron-barred receptacles held an assortment of slaves. They were well enough dressed for slaves, the girls in tissue-thin vestments and strings of cheap jewels, the men oiled and shaved, other men, of a variety of races, although unarmed unmistakable mercenary guards. They all looked miserable, as slaves look downcast; but they appeared well fed.

A voice called, "Splendid, jikai. Now let us out of here, in the name of Hiscielo the Chuns."

"Whoever he might be," I said to myself, and went across to the cage from which the woman called.

I knocked the lock off with a single blow. That is always a fine spirited—and empty—gesture. As soon as I'd committed that extravagant act of folly I checked the Krozair longsword, just in case. . . . The edge was unmarked from the iron. Which, given the art of the Krozair swordsmiths, was as it should be.

The woman said, "So, jikai, you prefer your sword to me?"

Prepared to be gracious to a gracious lady, I contented myself with a churlish: "Perhaps."

Well, she was beautiful. There was a kind of mesmeric force attached to her beauty. Everything about her appeared to be perfect, and that, very often—not always—adds up to a lack of perfection in the totality. Her hair was bright gold, long and rippling free over a turquoise dress girdled with gold. Her figure would take the breath away from any man who has not seen my Delia. Beside my Delia, this beautiful shining woman looked artificial. She was overwhelmingly aware of her personal attraction, for the force of her beauty, and the power that beauty confered.

She smiled alluringly at me. Her teeth were very white—they would have to be, seeing the list of perfections she possessed—and her lips were of that melting red that gets in under a fellow's ribs and twists about like a white-hot knife.

I made her a small bow. I was still wrought up, with the smoking corpses of dismembered men casually tumbled about.

"My lady—"

"You call me majestrix."

"So you're Queen Mab, then?"

She smiled.

"Release my servants. We must leave here at once."

I used more caution in opening the first cage holding a fat fellow with three quivering chins and a pot belly, garbed in black and green and with a great golden chain around his neck. I remembered the pit where we had freed Milsi.

"Open up the rest, dom," I said, and ignored his affronted dignity. The queen merely smiled.

Yet, in that smile, I thought I sensed rather than saw a puzzlement, as though she could not understand my attitude.

She couldn't grasp why I hadn't been bowled over by her beauty.

Well, people like her no doubt bathed in blood every day. A few poor fellows butchered meant nothing to her. . . .

As though carrying on that thought, she said, "You fight exceeding well."

"When I have to."

She frowned and the lightning flashed. "Majestrix!"

Her own guards were crowding out now and running to pick up the malko's fallen weapons. I had no desire to get into another fight. "Majestrix," I said dutifully.

She smiled.

Then I realized what the smile was for—it was certainly attractive, lighting up her face, as they say—it was designed to render me totally her slave, bound to her by adoration of her beauty. I did not laugh. I wasn't that far sunk in boorishness, by Vox!

She said, "Anglar! Move everybody out. We go that way." And she pointed to the black door at the end. So, the black door was the way we all went, fussed over by our fat friend in the black and green, and the chins, and the gold chains, Anglar the majordomo.

The corridors through which we walked were wide and well-lit, only a little dusty, and quite free of traps.

Feeling in no mood for conversation, I replied when spoken to and nothing else. She grew a little restive.

"You ask me nothing of this place. Have you been here long?"

I had to bite my lips to keep from shouting with mirth.

I eyed the guards she employed. They were all hulking great fellows, of a variety of races, and they carried weapons, and although I could probably put up a good show, I had no desire to fight them. So, because of that, I did not reply, as I ached to do, "Do you come here often?"

Mind you, by the disgusting diseased left eyeball of Makki-Grodno, had I done so, things might have turned out a little differently, by Zair!

Probably because of that feeling that I was reacting in a typically boorish way to a woman too conscious of her own powers of beauty and rank, and wishing to make amends, I said, "Majestrix. I am covered in the blood of those poor malkos, and I, perhaps, offend you. I must clean up as soon as possible."

And she said, "Jikai—you are very dear to me as you are. Do not fret."

Unable to make anything of this, or unwilling, I managed to mumble something and we walked on. In the next chamber we found a series of mangificently spread tables laid ready for us. And, in a small room in the corner, a bath.

I washed myself clean. I gave no thought to the oddness of finding a bath, where before we had traveled in our own muck, sweat and others' blood. . . .

She had prepared a chair next to hers, on her left hand, a chair smothered in chavonth pelts and ling furs, a chair almost like a throne. It was not, I saw as I sat down, quite so bountifully supplied with the symbols of rank as the chair in which she sat. The food smelled wonderful, looked marvelous and tasted delicious. It was, without question, superior to any food I'd come across before in the Coup Blag.

She spoke with her mouth full of basted chicken leg.

"You called those diabolical warrior malkos 'poor malkos' after they tried to slay you. They are very fierce. Do you feel guilt over their deaths?"

"Yes."

"But why?" She sipped wine, a red superior vintage, and swallowed. "They are fit for carrion."

"They are guards, paid to do a job."

"And are you paid to do a job?"

"I have been, in my time."

She leaned back against the pelts, and poked into her mouth with a bejeweled little finger. She spat a scrap of meat. Then she remembered.

She sat up.

"And you call me majestrix! Do not forget."

I said, "I will not forget, majestrix, if you do not."

For an instant I thought I'd gone too far. Then she smiled. That smile was a marvel, truly!

"I forgive you. I have never met a man like you before."

By Krun! If platitudes had been invented on Kregen, which they were not, she would have been first in the line.

It occurred to me that she would be pleased if I told her I'd never met a woman like her before. As this was almost true, I compounded the lie and told her. Her smile dazzled.

"Yes. I know. I am something special. . . ."

"Oh, yes," I said, taking up a deep rosé with just a hint of purple around the edges of the goblet. "Very special. Something quite else again."

And, as I thus foolishly ate and drank and tried to think of what to do next, I gave no heed to what was actually taking place around me. All I could see was a queen, and with her her retainers and guards, supping well. We had a walk to go before we escaped. But we would escape, I was certain.

As I say, I overlooked the most elementary of questions.

I offer in my exculpation only that the horror of this place must have worked on me, that I was worried over the fate of Seg and Milsi and the others, that I was tired—well, no, being tired is a sin, and I have no truck with it.

She said, "I had a map, a certain route through the Coup Blag. But it was lost."

Still no alarum bells tingled in my stupid old vosk skull of a head. This Queen Mab quite clearly knew what she was about, was used to wielding power, and I felt a dim stirring of surprise that so powerful a party as hers had been taken up. At least, our group were still free. . . . At least, at the least—I hoped and prayed they were.

"I think," she said. "I think I shall enjoy walking with you."

Very gallantly, waving the goblet aloft, I said, "And I with you, majestrix."

So, off we set again. There was a marked absence of traps in the corridors and rooms. I mentioned this. Two rooms later three of the guards were squashed against the roof as a stone block in the floor reared up on springs. Queen Mab just looked, tut-tutted, and we walked past on the other side.

She talked in a fine free way, animated, a flush across her cheeks. She displayed a queenly indifference to the horrors in this place. As we walked and talked, and what I said remains mostly a mystery to me—mainly a pack of lies about the romance and thrill of being a wandering adventurer and pak-tun—she would say, "Just so," and, "I see," and look suitably wise, bending her head graciously.

The slave girls in their silks and bangles looked bedraggled, and dragged their feet. Noticing this, I remarked that we were all tired, and that I hadn't slept in a long time. At once she lifted her hands in the air, looking toward her servants. Then she half-turned, halting, to look at me. At the time we were passing through a dim chamber suffused with a wan greenish light, and stuffed with piled coffins, from which stray wisps of cloth and desiccated limbs protruded.

"Tired? Oh, of course they are." She lowered her hands to her sides in a helpless gesture. "The poor things."

"We'll all march the better for a rest, majestrix."

"Most certainly. But let us find a more pleasing chamber than this."

The corridor, only a little dusty, turned and we walked up an incline. The next room, which was duly prodded by guards in what I could only take as a perfunctory manner, yielded nothing save a giant stone statue of some multi-limbed beast, standing on one leg at the center and trying to reach, with his tentacular trunk, a bunch of hanging fruit. The thing was grotesque. We hurried past.

The next room opened out into a blaze of light from crystal chandeliers.

I looked up, gaping. I expected the things to break free and fall on our heads, trying to slash us to ribbons.

A gigantic bed, big enough for a regiment, occupied the center of the room, masked by hanging damasks. Sweet scents cloyed on the air. Tables were laid with fruits and evening meal delicacies, and wine stood in amphorae.

The queen clapped her hands.

"Rest, everyone. Take your ease."

Everyone immediately flopped down on the cushions and rugs strewn about the floor. I looked about.

"Guards?" I said. "Majestrix."

"Guards? Oh, of course. Anglar—set guards."

He bowed deeply, his black and green robes flapping. He flourished his ivory wand at a hulking great Chulik, whose tusks were set with diamonds. The Chulik looked savage.

"Nath the Kaktu! Set guards as commanded. Bratch!"

Nath the Kaktu bratched, bellowing fiercely at his men. They went off and lolled at the entrances to the chamber. I decided that I'd sleep lightly and keep my fist wrapped around my sword hilt.

Now some of the three or four-armed folk of Kregen, and some with tail hands, who look like apims as far as faces are concerned, have been known when down on their luck to dress as apims, with their extra arms hidden. They may then wander through bazaars and markets, looking all innocence, and use their extra hidden hands to seize food and goods from the stalls and secret them inside their capacious clothes. One has to watch for rogues like this everywhere.

So—one of the guards, who looked like an apim with bad teeth and a ferocious haircut, standing guard by a door opposite the head of the bed, twitched his tunic around under his armor. I glanced across, caught by the movement, and Queen Mab called to me, lazily, a husky note in her voice.

Immediately, I walked toward the enormous bed, not wishing to give gratuitous offense, and the guard was forgotten for the moment.

A young fellow was in the act of walking away from the bed curtains, which were half-drawn. His skin was a clear smooth bronze; he had a pretty face, with crinkly hair and a rosebud mouth, and he looked sulky. His sulkiness turned to a look of hot resentment as he passed me. I ignored him.

A group of the slave girls gathered at the foot of the bed and began playing musical instruments and singing. The slaves carried enough boxes and bales to explain the instruments as well as the sumptuous clothes the queen wore. You may judge of my condition, a condition obscured from me at the time, when I say that I found the music enjoyable.

Now Delia can play the harp like an angel. Often of an evening in Esser Rarioch we would have musical sessions, and Jilian Sweet tooth would play her flute. Jilian is an accomplished flautist, and Delia's friends would gather and play and sing and we'd have a wonderful time. It was refined, of course, and very far from my evenings singing with the swods in taverns; but it was not ludicrous. Aimee could play a Kregen instrument not unlike a zither and the harmonies the ladies produced would have charmed birds out of trees. If I have not mentioned Aimee before it is only that she has not figured in my more hectic adventures up until a little later on.

So, now, I sat on the edge of the bed and listened to the music and enjoyed it, even though they performed that miserable song out of Hamal, "Black is the River and Black Was Her Hair." This is so painful as to be farcical.

The extent of that bed was truly amazing. The coverlet shone silkly, the pillows resembled the thighs of romance, the hanging tapestries and damasks glowed with amorous scenes. I watched as the music finished and the queen ordered her people to leave. Leaving that bed was like departing from a room of itself. The last hanging dropped into place and we were alone in the subdued glow of the lamps.

Well, she looked magnificent, like a wild beast of the jungle about to leap on her prey. She wore her golden hair loose, waving down in deep folds about her naked shoulders. The robe clung narrowly to her waist, slit from throat to ankle, and the golden lace blazed against her pale skin. Her mouth formed a luscious circle as she pouted at me. She stretched out a naked arm.

"Jikai—I am waiting."

Well, now. . . .

Judge of my condition when I found myself advancing upon her across the wide expanse of the bed. Oh, yes! I, Dray Prescot, savage wild leem of a fellow, moving in on this delectable woman who lay back, pillowed in her golden hair, as the robe parted. It was all beyond belief.

The thought of Delia sprang into my mind, and the queen said, "You have loved before, jikai, I can tell. But they were nothings. Mere trifles. I own that I am surprised—"

I swallowed. Her perfume dizzied me. She was really beautiful, now, I could see that, beautiful and desirable.

The way her skin flushed delicately with rose, the way her body curved, the way her mouth pouted, red and shining with passion. . . .

"Surprised?" I managed to stammer out. "I am surprised—"

"You should not be. I am irresistible! My surprise is for myself, that I have formed so violent an attachment for you."

A roaring thundered in my head. There was only the body of the queen in the whole wide world of Kregen before my eyes. I inched closer, and now I was crawling over that silky coverlet. She lifted her naked arms, white and pink against the blaze of her hair.

"Irresistible! No man can resist me, not even you, Dray Prescot!"

"Majestrix," I mumbled.

"I am tormented with longing for you," she went on, her face flushing now, her body rising as I neared her. "I am prepared to—no matter—you are the luckiest man alive . . ."

She was very sure of herself. Well, she had every right to be. She *was* delectable. And she was arrogant with her power, conscious of her sway. Women have this power, it is undeniable. They use it; that, too, cannot be gainsaid. No doubt they boast of their conquests, woman to woman, in their private moments. I cannot stand a man who talks about women, and I usually withdraw when men start their boring conquest stories. As for women who boast to men. . . .

The image of Delia rose before me, scalding.

I stopped moving forward.

She saw. Her face lengthened, her eyes brightened in the lamplight, her gaze fastening on me like the teeth of a shark, a remora, leaching away.

Two things happened, one a memory, the other a move-

ment. I truly believe and would stake my immortal ib on
it—I saw through her and jerked back before those two
events occurred.

One—the memory—was what she had called me, without a
Llahal or the pappattu between us.

The other—the movement—an insolent brown and red
scorpion waddled out from under the pillows and stood, balanced, waving his stinger at the lush and naked body of the
queen.

Saved by the bell?

No!

Saved because I understood all too tardily just what went
forward here. And, then, many men would not call it being
saved; they'd call me all kinds of benighted idiot. But I
knew—and could guess—and in that moment the full horror
hit me.

She saw the scorpion.

She screamed.

That scorpion was real to her, if not to me, real and not a
part of the mumbojumbo.

She was off the bed and scrabbling for the curtains and
they parted as Anglar thrust in, and, with him, the bulky
form of the Chulik, Nath the Kaktu. Anglar swept a massive
green and black cloak about the woman, massive in that it
concealed her body and hooded up over her head and turned
her into another being. The golden hair fell away, ripped
free. Dark hair, dark and shining, swooping down to a peak
over her forehead lay revealed. Her face blanched with
vicious temper.

She stood and a trembling finger pointed at me.

"I shall not slay you, Dray Prescot. You resist me now.
But you will submit—you *shall* submit! If it takes all your
life, you shall submit!"

I said, "I do not know who you are. You are not Queen
Mab. But I do not know you."

"You will, Dray Prescot, you will!"

I took a breath. The spell was broken. I said, "You seem to
call me by a name you know. How is that?"

"Fool!"

"Well," I said, equably, "that is true, and I do not deny it.
You say you have formed an attachment for me. That is your
misfortune, woman, for you should know better—"

"Beware—"

"Oh, I'll beware all right. You are not Pancresta, that is sure. But you know of Spikatur Hunting Sword?"

Anglar laughed. Even the Chulik, polishing up his tusk, grimaced—and Chuliks and a sense of humor are light-years apart.

"I know of the creeping worms! Spikatur! We took them over, and made them do our will—*our* will! And you, you ruined it all, you and your wizards! I know! Why I do not condemn you to a life of torment I cannot say—" She put a hand to her forehead, a white naked arm snaking from the black and green robe. She looked suddenly bewildered.

I looked for my ally, the scorpion, but he had vanished.

The curtains of the bed parted as Anglar and Nath the Kaktu assisted this woman to step away from the bed and out to her chair. This thronelike chair was pushed into a cleared space. I crawled off the end of the bed and thought to take up the Krozair longsword from where I'd shed it as I'd gone slinking forward under the spell of this woman. For, spell it truly was.

And then! By Zair, I tell you, my heart turned over and all the blood rushed to my head and I was almost sick, sick as any poor beaten cur dog. . . .

A tinkling tintinabulation of golden bells. . . .

The woman closed her eyes, sitting erect in the thronelike chair. Her eyelids were covered in gold leaf, and not unusually in the way of that kind of cosmetic fad, the leaf split along the lines of creases. In that moment all the beauty of her face dissipated, so that the pallor of her skin and the golden eyelids resembled a corpse face, painted for the last death journey to the Ice Floes of Sicce.

The multitude of tiny bells tinkled and tingled, and I felt the blood rush from my heart.

Stiffly, I turned about. A procession entered the crystal chandelier-lit chamber. A familiar, a horribly familiar, a blasphemous procession. . . .

"You fool," whispered the woman, naked in her green and black robe. "What you have thrown away. . . ."

Instead of sixteen Womoxes, bulking in their black tabards girt with green lizard skin, horns all gilded, there were but twelve. They bore a palanquin smothered in decoration and with its golden cloth of gold and embroidered curtains half-drawn. Against the red-gold sliding gleam of silks within a small shape showed, in shadow. The massed golden bells, tiny, spine-chilling, tinkled into the enveloping silence.

There were Katakis in the procession, savage, evil, preda-
tory men, slavemasters with their low-drawn brows and snag-
gly teeth. Their whiptails curled boldly above their
black-haired heads, and each tail was strapped with bladed
steel. There were Chail Sheom, beautiful half-naked girls,
chained and decorated, painted, whimpering. There were all
manner of strange and obscene creatures, fashioned from
nightmare, not of the Kregen I knew. There were, in this procession, things I had not seen before, and there were things
missing.

The voice I had heard in that room of the blue doors, that
had, all but one, turned red, whispered now.

"Mother," said that fragile voice. "Why do you tarry?
What ails you?"

The woman opened her eyes. They were now of a deep
pellucid green. I looked from her to the procession, and the
palanquin, and tried to discern the creature within.

I remembered the warning, burned into the portal of the
Coup Blag. But he was dead! He had been blown away in the
Quern of Gramarye. He had to be—he was dead, dead, dead!

"You—" I choked out. "You are dead!"

"Silence, Dray Prescot." The woman spoke on a hiss, my
name long-drawn with evil, and yet, and yet—she looked at
me with those green depthless eyes, and I shuddered.

"Mother—we have won—why do you wait?"

So, then, I saw it, or thought I did, and trembled anew for
the fresh evil loosed upon the glorious and forbidding world
of Kregen.

Again I tried to peer past the cloth of gold curtains into
the interior of the palanquin. Man or woman, boy or girl?
How tell, in that eerie whispering voice?

Then, among the retinue of people following the palanquin
I saw Pancresta, walking not proudly, but in a resigned,
shoulder-drooping way. And I saw that we had been de-
ceived. Spikatur Hunting Sword, we had been told, had been
taken over by some new leader, some person with fresh ideas
for evil and murder. And I thought I knew who that person,
that devil, was; and yet I knew I did not know.

For Phu-Si-Yantong was dead.

He was not in that palanquin, so like the one I had seen
him ride in before. He was a mighty Wizard of Loh; I did not
think he could come back from the grave.

The woman must have read a deal of the apalled thoughts

on my face. Truth to tell, by Zair, I am not sure what I thought, what I imagined, in that moment of horror.

"Yes, Dray Prescot. Yes. You are trapped. My child rides in the palanquin that was my own and only wizard's. You and your vile sorcerous friends slew my wizard. I tried to aid him and could not. You have much to answer for, and yet, and yet. . . ."

"Mother!" The weird whispering voice, so like its father's voice, sharpened. Still I could not tell if the creature borne within the palanquin was wizard or witch. "Mother! The time is now. We have played the game well, and we have joyed in it. But, mother—*now!*"

Yes, they'd played their games with me. The woman had given me no Llahal when we met, and not inquired my name, had not, in her impersonation of the queen that I had fostered, inquired for news of the king. She had known. She had known all there was to know about this place from the beginning, for she and her wizard, Phu-Si-Yantong, had constructed it themselves.

No wonder the power of this place was wielded with such consummate ease!

I had to hold onto the fact that I was not dealing with Yantong. The child in the palanquin was aping her—or his—father. The woman was speaking again.

"My name, Dray Prescot, is Csitra. Mark it well. I owed you a score such as any woman would hunger to avenge. Yet I would have spared you, as you know. I would have raised you up, against the wishes of my child, the child of Phu-Si-Yantong. Know, now, that I, Csitra, am a Witch of Loh, and you are doomed!"

Chapter Twenty

A Voice Speaks

I found a voice. If it was my voice, or another's, if it spoke from the grave, or from my love for Delia, if it was fostered by some lingering aftereffect of the counter-spells worked on me by my comrade Wizards of Loh, I did not know. If it came from the Star Lords I did not know. That, even then, seemed to me so unlikely as to be a foolish wisp of a whim.

That voice issuing from my throat spoke up bravely.

"Now wait a minute!" said the voice. "Now, just hold on—hold on a moment! You say you would have spared me, would have raised me up—and this after what you say was done to your wizard. Well, and what have I—here and now—said or done that offends you? Tell me, Csitra the Witch, tell me—if you can!"

"What—" She put a hand, again, to her head.

The long golden hair she had worn as part of her disguise, when I had forced on her, by my assumption, the identity of Queen Mab, lay abandoned. Her own shining black hair, peaked over her forehead, sweeping tightly past her ears, suited her better. Her beauty remained; but now in a strange and, indeed, frightening way, the artificiality had vanished. She was herself, Csitra, and the depth of terror was—she looked and was the better favored for that.

"What do you mean?"

"Mother! Waste no more time. The tormentors await and I must slake my just vengeance first!"

Her head rolled from side to side. Her voice faltered. "Phunik! Wait, wait—there is more here—"

"The man is mortal, he is Dray Prescot, and he is doomed! *Queyd-arn-tung!*"

That means no more need be said, but more did need to be said, and said damned quick.

I found that voice speaking again. "Since when does a

164

mother, even a witch, sit still under insults from her own child? I have not insulted you. I treated you with courtesy—"

"You slew my wizard!"

"That," said the voice, "was before I met you."

"Do you know, Dray Prescot, what you are saying?"

A shrewd question. I did not. But I was in no condition to argue. I went on with that voice issuing from my mouth: "I have known very few Witches of Loh. I detest braggarts, pushy people, the vainglorious of the world. Perhaps had I known you were a Witch of Loh, and not a mere queen, I would have understood. Do you, Csitra the Witch, understand that?"

I, myself, was under no delusions. I was fighting for my life. Instead of cold steel, I used a voice and a tongue that welled up from some unsuspected source of deceit deep within me. And, anyway, of what use a warrior's sword against a witch's spell?

"Mother!"

Her green gaze left me and centered on the palanquin.

"Wait, my uhu, wait."

So, now, I understood what the creature in the palanquin was. Uhu—a hermaphrodite, half man, half woman, a person cursed or blessed with androgynous characteristics that could make its, hers or his life a heaven or a hell—uhu.

"Why, mother, why?"

"Because I say so!"

And the green eyes blazed with an awful occult power.

Asinine, my remark—rather, the remark of the voice issuing from my mouth. "Young, the uhu?"

"Yes, Dray Prescot. Young and unformed, a coy among wizardly witches. But able to destroy you—if I please."

"But why—*now*—should that please you? You see I do not prevaricate. I am what I am, what the gods fashioned me. I mistook you. That was a mistake, but an understandable one. What is past is past. Even a witch cannot alter that."

"You think so?"

I refused to rise to that bait.

I felt the cold in me. I was shivering. If talk could keep me alive, I'd talk the four hind legs off a vove.

She looked at me as though I were a frog's leg, to be dissected. "How can I trust you?"

I breathed a shaky breath. Those words told me I had won a small space, a tiny moment of time in which to operate.

The uhu from the palanquin spat out vicious, tumbling

words, adding up to a demand that I be handed over—instantly.

"Phunik," said Csitra the Witch. "A flyer remains unsaddled." Which is to say that there is unfinished business. "Leave me. Go and play with your creatures. I will call when I have decided—"

"Mother!"

"Go, my uhu, go."

She turned her shoulder to the palanquin and the retinue of grotesque and ghastly retainers mingled with the chained slave girls and the warrior guards.

The moment hung charged with tensions that I, a mere mortal man, would never comprehend. It seemed to me the crystal chandeliers twined together and rushed upon me. The sweetly scented air cloyed and tried to suffocate me. The very floor rolled like a leaky seventy-four after four years' blockade off Brest. I saw the people staring at the palanquin, at the witch, and at me. I thought I would fall from the clamor in my head.

After three or four centuries of black emptiness, the tiny golden bells began to tinkle, and the procession turned around, and the Womoxes lifted the palanquin. Sheened in red-gold, glittering, and yet black with an indrawn power, the palanquin bearing the uhu, Phunik, the child of Phu-Si-Yantong and the Witch of Loh, Csitra, moved away out of my sight. I saw it go. I did not believe it had gone, not really; but the witch and I were left alone with her own people.

"Now, Dray Prescot, I think you must prove to me in deeds what you say in words."

Overcoming the first spell of allurement she had placed on me had been accomplished only through my Delia, and the scorpion, and my own wits. Could I hope to defeat a second and far stronger spell?

The chamber with its dangling chandeliers spun about me. I felt the nausea rising. I fell down. I, Dray Prescot, Lord of Strombor and Krozair of Zy, fell down in a faint. Well, to be honest, I performed the fainting act well; but that act needed little assistance, by Krun! Like any poor unfortunate girl cramped into too-tight clothes and paying the penalty for fashion, I fainted away.

As I toppled to the ground, I remember thinking that the girls who fainted to order were rather cleverer than stupid . . .

Cold logic—now—makes me sweat in retrospect. She

could so easily have thrown a spell of true cognizance upon
me and so suspected that I but shammed. Her slaves lifted
me up and bore me off, and she cooed and aahed over me,
with my poor lamb this and my poor dove that as to make
the nausea rise almost uncontrollably in my guts. But I held
fast, and was carted off.

In my struggle against Phu-Si-Yantong I had always imagined and hoped that there was in the wizard a streak of good-
ness. I had found it difficult to believe that any man, Wizard
of Loh or not, could be entirely evil. So, now, I fancied that
in this witch-woman, Csitra, some tenderness for others than
herself or the objects of her desire must exist.

I profoundly hoped so.

All the same, until I had been revived I was of no use to
her. She called for someone named Pamantisho the Beauty,
and heard an answering shout of joy and the quick patter of
feet. That would be the pretty boy who had passed me with
so sullen an expression. Csitra the Witch would be occupied
for a bur or two, then. . . .

No doubt the length of time I had to plan and execute my
escape depended on pretty boy Pamantisho's staying power.

Having had no orders either to bind me or knock me about
a bit, the guards just dumped my lax body onto a pile of
cushions in a corner. They talked among themselves, and I
gathered they were not happy here, and those few from Loh
wanted to get back there very quickly. They said they were
going for some booze—their words were highly colorful—and
then they might hunt up some fun elsewhere. Guards in a
witch's retinue ought to be superfluous. What their fun would
be I did not care to guess.

I cracked an eyelid open.

It goes without saying that when a warrior falls down in a
faint he will grip tenaciously onto what he is holding. The
guards had passed a few uncomplimentary remarks about the
longsword; but it was still there, and someone had tucked it
down into the scabbard. I did not think this merited any comment on the quality of guards Csitra employed; they did their
job and no doubt were paid, and they had seen the witch's
powers, and tthe way she and I had, at the end, got on.

Now I was about to test the witch's powers again. . . .

The guards began some of the usual warrior nonsense
down at the wine tables, and others shouted at them to shut
up, Shastum! and then someone shied an empty goblet at a
chandelier.

This appeared a typical scene. For me, it represented just about the only chance I'd get.

So, now, I had to stand up, get out of here—and run.

By Krun!

I wanted to lie there. Just to lie there and rest. My body felt as though a sixteen-ton weight had rolled back and forth along the length of my spine. My eyes were red raw. My mouth was like—well like some disgusting part of some disgusting creature's anatomy. I just wanted to lie there and go to sleep.

Metaphorically, the snowflakes whirled about me and the deep snow formed my couch and pillow, and I could close my eyes and drift off, peacefully and gently and wonderfully.

No. Not good enough, not for a craggy old Krozair of Zy who had comrades to think of, and a world to save, and Delia at the end. . . . My joints sounded like frozen twigs going bang bang bang under the iron hooves of horses. I stood up. I nearly fell down. And then, somehow, I was in at the back of a hanging arras, and breathing dust and cobwebs, and feeling my way along the rough stone wall.

By this time there was just me, a scarlet breechclout and a Krozair longsword. All the rest of my gaudy trappings had vanished.

With a scarlet breechclout and a Krozair brand a fellow is as well dressed and equipped as he needs to be, save at the poles, on that marvelous and terrifying world of Kregen.

Along corridors and passageways, avoiding traps, stumbling across rooms where specters gibbered, climbing stairs where the decomposing corpses of unfortunates told of sprung traps, hauling myself along by willpower, I dragged a painful way. Do not ask me if I would have escaped. I try not to boast, for, as I had told Csitra, I do detest the braggarts and pushy people of two worlds. Perhaps I would have been caught and moldered away in a fiendish trap, or been melted down in an acid bath, or been chewed up in the fangs of a monstrous beast from nightmare.

But, somehow or other, there is in my thick old vosk-skull of a head the fixed idea that I would have escaped.

I think that being a Krozair of Zy played a major part in that thinking. Poor old Phu-Si-Yantong—he'd come unstuck before against a Krozair Brother. It was quite clear that no Brother of any Order of Krozairs had been through this maze before.

But the people of Spikatur Hunting Sword had.

Down low on the corner of a doorway the sign, cut into the stone, showed the heart pierced by a line. That line not only showed direction, it was the sword, the sword piercing the heart that was the sign of Spikatur Hunting Sword.

Staggering, making a sketchy attempt to prod the floor with my own sword, and glaring up with bloodshot eyes at the roof and around the walls, I tottered on. I followed the sign, the sign of Spikatur, and I followed it back the way we had come.

How long would it be before the uhu, Phunik, tired of playing with his creatures? How long before Csitra wearied of her amorous sport? Then they could go into lupu and descry objects at a distance. They could use the signomants they must have located in the corridors and tunnels. Then they would see me. Their vengeance would be swift.

Stumbling, I staggered on through rooms I recognized.

The carved doorway through which we had entered could not now be far off.

With great caution I entered a circular chamber. There were twelve doors, paneled and colored. Halfway around the chamber lay the mummified corpses of two werstings and two strigicaws with slit throats. Opposite them, near a splay of bones and skulls, the body of a Chulik sat propped against the wall. Of the hellhounds and the Pachak there was no sign.

I breathed with an open mouth, panting, my eyes wild, my hair falling over my forehead, gulping for breath. The Krozair longsword in my fist trembled.

The streaming mingled lights of Zim and Genodras, the Twin Suns of Scorpio, never reached down into this subterranean gloom. The crystal shed its radiance upon the scene. Under the Suns the Wizards of Kregen flourish, and are of many kinds. Some pretend to powers they yearn for and may never attain. Others make little show and can blast you where you stand. Some are not yet in possession of the secrets of thaumaturgical art they will later acquire. I had known Wizards of Loh who had been successfully kept prisoner by barbarians, by maniacal lords, probably because those Wizards of Loh did not number among their arcane arts those of blasting and destruction. Some, whom I had rescued, had later learned the awful secrets.

Most Wizards of Loh could go into lupu and see at a distance. I sweated and gazed about, seeking the doorway through which our party had first entered here. The feeling of unseen eyes watching me oppressed me with a palpable weight.

We had uncovered the mystery of Spikatur. Originally formed to combat the crazed schemes of Hamal in the person of poor old mad Empress Thyllis, Spikatur would have ceased to exist once Hamal had been defeated and was now being reconstructed. The conspiracy had been taken over and given a new and darker impetus. Once powerful forces containing our own wizards came to the Coup Blag, this place would no longer support those who directed Spikatur Hunting Sword. By Sasco, no!

In those whirling moments of darkness as I stumbled across the chamber, heading for a way out and into the light of day, I felt the absolute conviction that Seg Segutorio would win through. He would not lose his life down here. He would succeed. Good old Seg!

I could see the door I wanted. The sword piercing the heart wavered as my gaze faltered. Everything was going up and down. I staggered on.

The door opened.

Things rushed through, a crazed cloud of kaotim, Undead, decomposed corpses shedding their grave wrappings, skeletons clicking and clanking, beasts and half-beasts, risen from the tomb to sink their spectral fangs into me.

Shuddering, I threw the longsword up before my face.

If this was to be the last fight, it would be a fight, by Zair. . . .

Without waiting for the revolting mass of Undead to reach me, I let rip a long ululating scream and raced forward, sword flaming, ripped into them in a wild surge of fury and despair.

Yet, despair? ·That charge was wild and ferocious, an onslaught of murderous precision. The Krozair brand sliced and hacked, bits and pieces of corpse flew, bones sundered and crunched to powder. The things whirled about me. Yet, fiendish though it was in sheer blattering headlong fury, my charge was aimed. Hacking a way through, I did not stop. I cut and slashed and went on, unstoppable, heading for the door I needed.

There was no slaughter here, for these foul creatures were already dead. In that breakneck onset I merely sent them back to where they had shambled from. Strange, too, to witness the superb Krozair longsword slicing and cutting and bursting gross bodies asunder and remaining steel-bright and unsullied. Yellow bones cracked and flew into spouting chips. Sere skulls gaped emptily at me, and cracked open as one cracks an egg open with a spoon, and nothingness gusted out. . . .

Only a few long paces separated me from the door. With a howl of such savage ferocity as would wake the dead, if they were not already awakened, I burst through the last of the kaotim. A single smashing backhanded blow and I was through the door.

To slam it shut was the work of an instant and then I hared on tottering legs along the corridor. I could recall the layout—I could dodge the traps—I could take the correct twists and turns, and fight my way through the miasmic spirit-sucking atmosphere of this place. I could!

Mind you, memory ducks and dimples hereabouts. I recall some of the passageways and I think—I am almost certain—there appeared a pair of Kataki twins who were left in four or five pieces. But that could have been a dream. I thundered on.

I came to the foot of an enormous spiral staircase. I gulped air, tasting the flat stale dustiness of it where there was no real dust upon the floor, and started up.

What I expected, I do not know. Surely, by this time, Csitra or her uhu, Phunik, must have disengaged themselves and be watching me? Perhaps they continued to play their wicked games. They had turned Spikatur Hunting Sword to their own ends, and been discovered. Their pleasures were of the dark and ghastly kinds. They but toyed with me, I thought, and then came out to the top of the stairs and so hurried through the corridors. No, they could not be free yet, could not be spying on me, I thought, and tried the passageways and so came to the last chamber. Here we had all entered in, apprehensively, boldly, fearfully, but we had all gone in. And the Pachaks had entered cheerfully, lusting after plunder. I was glad they were still with Seg. More than ever I was confident he would get out safe, alive and well.

The radiance of jade and ruby, streaming in through the archway!

Ah! The supreme blessedness of the Suns of Scorpio, shining refulgently, beckoning me on!

Outside lay the jungle. That was a mere nothing to a man in my mood, a man who had dared the dangers of the Coup

Blag and beaten them. I'd swing through the forest to freedom.

I would have, too. . . . I am confident of it. . . .

Mouth open, hair flying, limbs aching, eyes glaring, I stumbled on toward that beckoning radiance.

The brilliance of Zim and Genodras thickened and tinged with blue.

The blueness grew about me, dazzling me and a chill touched my skin. I gaped upward. Hovering, bloating, enormous, the outline of a Scorpion, radiantly blue, leered down upon me.

"No!" was all I could gasp before I was sucked up and whirled away through unguessable dimensions.

I opened my eyes.

I was sitting in a chair, and the chair, hissing, rushed along a lighted corridor. But I knew I was in no corridor of the Coup Blag.

I unfurled my tongue and wet my lips and managed to husk out: "Star Lords!"

The chair rushed around a corner and into a wide room. It hissed. It swiveled. It deposited me before a blank wall, and stopped, and I remained, sitting. It is most unlikely, whatever the necessity, that I could have stood up.

A voice: "Dray Prescot."

"I know that," I said. And, then, I thought to say: "The Shanks. They have reached Paz?"

"Not yet. There is time. There are things you must witness."

"Aye," I said. "There are things I *have* witnessed!"

"If you are to serve both your will and ours, if you are to save Paz, watch and listen."

I opened my mouth, but the effort was too great, and I closed it again, clamping my black-fanged winespout shut, and I watched as light bloomed on the wall before me.

By Beng Dikkane, the patron saint of all the ale-drinkers of Paz! I could do with a wet right now!

The glow grew like an unfolding flower. The light showed me a picture within the flower shape, a picture of color and movement and sound, and thought. I stared and listened, enthralled.

"You see what may happen, Dray Prescot."

Seg! Seg Segutorio, and with him Milsi, and Kalu and his Pachaks, and Fregeff! And complaining old Exandu, helped along by Shanli, with Hop the Intemperate to look out for them. They moved along a stone corridor, and the radiance of the suns lay before them.

"Thank Opaz!" I said.

"Remember, what you see is only what may happen."

"It will. . . . It will!"

And then the weirdness of hearing the inner thoughts of the people in the picture overcame me. Seg was tortured by guilt—guilt over abandoning me—and yet in his thoughts the strong belief shone through that he knew of me, as I knew of him, that we would both soldier through.

And Milsi's thoughts overcame me also, and I hungered for Seg to know the truth.

And the others. . . . I shut my mind to their thoughts. This was eavesdropping! This was contemptuous invasion of privacy! This was, this was—

"It is necessary, Dray Prescot, onker of onkers, that you *know*."

"Know what?"

"Know what it is needful for you to know. No more."

"I needn't really have asked, need I?"

And then all the foolishness was swept away.

The picture changed.

The voice said, "This has happened, this is smoke blown with the wind."

I saw a small and secret chamber banked with flowers. I could smell the scents, heady, intoxicating. A woman sat at a low table, gracious in the way she bent to untie the last thong on her calf-high boots. She was garbed in hunting leathers of russet, and propped against the table stood a rapier and scabbarded to the other end of the belt and lying on the table, lay the matching main gauche. A shimmer moved all across the picture and now the woman, still with her back to me, was dressed all in sheerest white. Her shining brown hair fell softly in gentle waves, her form dizzied me. She lifted her arms to unfasten the white gown, and I realized that time must have passed since the moment, a mere heartbeat or two ago, that I had first seen her. A night had passed in that short interval.

She turned to face me.

Yes—yes!

I had known, known from the first moment I had seen her. And now my Delia smiled, that smile that can twist me up and wring me out and deposit me like a limp dishrag at her feet—when she chooses. She smiled in welcome.

"You know I must leave you now? I wish it were otherwise, but—"

She spoke to another person in that secret flower-bowered room. The shadow moved across the table as the other person approached.

A fierce voice said, "I know you must leave, and I hate it!"

"I have to, so no more need be said. And I am late already."

A man moved into the picture, his back to me, and all I could see was a hulking great fellow, naked to the waist, with the muscles like boa constrictors, and a stupid yellow breechclout. I stared. I tasted ashes.

Delia said, "You will not fret when I am gone—no, no—of course you will. Well, now you know what it is like."

And the man's obnoxious bellow said: "I know! But, before you change into your hunting russets, and your black boots, and do on your rapier and dagger, I think—my heart, I really do think there is time."

And Delia of the Blue Mountains, Delia of Delphond, laughed, delightfully mocking at the great hulking brute of a beast. She rose, glorious as a woman who knows she is a woman, and knows a woman's power and does not abuse that privilege. Splendid she was, so splendid as to catch the breath in the throat. Nothing else in two worlds mattered to me save Delia, and this ugly brute took her up in his arms as a leem might seize on its prey, and held her close; and I saw the way he held her, the gentleness and the tenderness so extraordinarily at odds with his appearance.

And so this—this person—swung Delia about and I saw his face.

And it was me.

So I remembered, this scene I was watching, recalled it with a pang as just one of the many many times Delia had gone off about her secret affairs for the Sisters of the Rose.

I collapsed back into the hissing chair of the Star Lords, and I shuddered. For I could sense the flowing thoughts as Delia mourned for the parting, mourned as I mourned, and we poor wights caught up in the toils of duty that sundered our paths. Pitiful, yes, of course; but there was more to this life of ours than that, a great deal more. . . .

"Watch, Dray Prescot," said the voice. "Watch and listen."

"Spikatur—"

"You have smoked out their lair. You know how they will be dealt with, how they must be dealt with. These pictures before you now, they are your new reality."

Wrought up as I was, bloody, tattered, exhausted, I could not leave alone the horrors through which I had been.

"And that uhu brat of Yantong's?"

"Shastum! That is to be. Watch and listen and learn!"

So I watched.

I watched as Delia, the Empress of Vallia, put on her russet hunting leathers, and pulled up her tall black boots. I saw the professional way she strapped her weapons about her: rapier and main gauche scabbarded at her sides, the Lohvian longbow built for her by Seg over one shoulder, the quiver of arrows, fletched with the superb crimson feathers of the zimkorf of Valka, angled cunningly to hand, the long narrow Valkan dagger down one boot. She disdained the cape the pictured representation of myself offered her, throwing her head back so that the lights caught and gleamed in those outrageous chestnut highlights in her hair, reckless, glowing, filled with life.

Had she been with Seg and me as we tramped through the Snarly Hills she would have been more dangerous than either of us, than both of us put together, I did not doubt, by Zair!

Sitting sunken in a daze of longing wonder, exhausted, I watched the pictures, fired with passion, shaking with fear, exhilarated beyond reason, as the moments passed.

I, Dray Prescot, watched and suffered and triumphed with my Delia, my Delia of the Blue Mountains, my Delia of Delphond.

The fate of our Vallia was being decided as I watched and hearkened, and through the terrors that near drove me insane with fear for Delia I saw how she marched so blithely along and I thought I understood a little more of what the Star Lords wished me to know.

What the Everoinye did was done with knowledge and forethought, and what few mistakes they might make had no effect whatsoever on their plans.

A table hissed up from somewhere and brought refreshments. I sat, sunken, gripped by terror for Delia, watching. At last, the picture died. I had touched nothing of the food and drink on the table.

When the enormous blue Scorpion of the Star Lords came

for me I cared nothing for Spikatur Hunting Sword, nothing for the Shanks. One thought, and one thought only, possessed me.

I stretched out my arms and soared into the blue infinity.